# Emmetyville 2

Jeremy Moorhouse

First published as paperback in Britain 2020

Copyright © Jeremy Moorhouse 2020

The right of Jeremy Moorhouse to be identified as the Author of the Work has been asserted by him in accordance with the Copyright, Designs and Patents Act 1988.

All rights reserved. No part of this publication may be reproduced, distributed, or transmitted in any form or by any means, including photocopying, recording, or other electronic or mechanical methods, without the prior written permission of the publisher, except in the case of brief quotations embodied in critical reviews and certain other non-commercial uses permitted by copyright law. For permission requests, write to
Jeremy Moorhouse, penguinpost60@googlemail.com

All persons in this publication are fictitious and any resemblance to real persons, living or dead is purely coincidental.

**ISBN:** 9798872230472

# DEDICATION

For my friends in Looe and Polperro, and everyone who works in coastal tourist towns all over the world.

Emmet, noun. Cornish word for Ant.

"We'm all cousins here"

Acknowledgements

So many people helped to make this possible, but special thanks must go to Helen, who was the unfortunate soul who had to listen to all my attempts at humour along the way.

# Easter.

Donald and Sylvia were making the most of the all-in breakfast. Compared to Donald, Sylvia had eaten quite modestly. At home they lived very differently. Sylvia usually breakfasted on porridge and Donald enjoyed two boiled eggs with plumbers. Most people called them soldiers, but Donald had worked for the water board until he had retired, and it was one of his little jokes.

So far, Donald had eaten a bowl of prunes and peaches, two bowls of cereal, a portion of kippers with a poached egg, a full English breakfast, and an astonishing six pieces of toast.
Sylvia was doing quite well herself, although she'd restricted herself to one bowl of cereal and passed on the kippers. Out of politeness, she'd opted for the smaller breakfast and politely asked for no baked beans. She reasoned that the prunes would probably do their work quite adequately without the additional bean fibre.

Breakfast was included in the price of their Easter break, and so they were determined to extract every ounce of value, even to the point where, when he thought no one was watching, Donald had stored extra slices of bread and rashers of bacon from the breakfast bar, into a plastic sandwich bag he'd brought with him for exactly that purpose.
He winked at Sylvia as he tucked his prize into the pocket of his jacket. Sylvia hoped the bag wouldn't leak grease on the linen. Donald had loved the jacket. She'd brought it home from the charity shop where she volunteered every Thursday afternoon. She knew she wasn't supposed to take

items from the donations, but on a Thursday, the manageress wasn't there, and Sylvia considered a few bits and pieces a fair exchange for her labour.

The waiter came to their table for what must have been the twelfth time that morning.

"Is everything okay Sir? Madam?"
He was momentarily distracted when, yet another walking stick clattered to the floor. He ought to have been used to it by now.

"Oh, it was lovely" Sylvia answered truthfully.
"Yes, super young man." Donald agreed with an approving nod. "Is there any coffee left?" he added, "with some of those nice biscuits?"

Paul was unsurprised, the same scene was repeating across the dining room as his colleagues catered to the needs of their valued guests. Every week a coachload of retired visitors would arrive for a four-day special. Because the coach trips were included in the price, the visitors seemed to think they were getting excellent value. Paul, on his steppingstone to full hotel management, had worked out the figures compared to the full main season price. Between the cost of the booking and the money spent at the bar and in the hotels shop, the owners of the hotel were making a handsome profit.
"Keep them happy, fill them up with breakfast and complimentary sherry, we'll get it all back on Cabaret night" the manager would coach his staff. Paul had seen just how well this tactic worked.

Donald sat back in his chair and stretched while Sylvia

burped as quietly as she could into her napkin. The motion of the coach had sent them both to sleep during the overnight drive, as it had most of their fellow breakfasting companions. It was the first time they'd had a real opportunity to observe the rest of the group.

A few people were beginning to leave the breakfast tables now. The sound of radio Cornwall from the dining room wall speakers, was temporarily obscured by the sound of chairs scraping, and a cacophony of sore knees and hips moans and groans. There was an assortment of voices all wondering where their walking sticks were or vocalising their desires that their hip operations would hurry up.

Most of the group appeared to be in their 60's or 70's. "Look at that lot." Donald, now 74, tilted his head with a sideways look "Strewth, what a load of old codgers, we must be the youngest ones here."
Sylvia, 73 a few days previously, nodded back in agreement and smiled appreciatively at Paul as the coffee arrived.

The couple who'd risen from the table next to them noticed what was happening and the eager woman clasped Paul's shoulder and said, "Oh, is there coffee love? We'll sit down again then." As Paul headed back to the barista she called after him, "and plenty of biscuits please love?"
She gestured at the table with her stick saying to her husband, "We'd better sit down again Norman, I'll see if I can get us a few packets of those biscuits for later."
Norman did as he was instructed, when Marjorie wanted something, she generally got it.

Now that they'd made eye contact with Donald and Sylvia, Norman leant forward and introduced himself and

Marjorie, and extended his hand. Donald quickly licked a dollop of marmalade from his hand before warmly reciprocating.

As they clasped hands, Norman tapped his thumb three times on the back of Donald's hand. Donald tapped back twice with his own thumb.
"A pleasure to meet you" Donald said, "and good to know you're on the square."

A bizarre exchange followed as they maintained eye contact.

"How old is your grandmother?" Norman asked Donald.
"She's 173, I see you have travelled to the east." Donald answered before asking "Are you a travelling man?"
"I am as it happens" Norman replied "I generally travel from east to west. Have you seen my dog, Hiram?"

"Oh look, the coffee, thank you." Norman thanked Paul and began chatting to Donald as he poured.

Marjorie looked at Sylvia and rolled her eyes.

"Oh these boys and their special club games."
Sylvia nodded in agreement as the men talked.
Sylvia didn't normally meet the partners of Donald's special club brethren. It would be nice to chat with Marjorie she thought, especially when Donald and Norman were out of the way. Sylvia was suspicious about what Donald and his friends got up to. Hopefully, Marjorie would know a lot more than she did. As they sipped their coffees, they were soon deeply engrossed in conversation too.

As he had discreetly cleared the breakfast things from the

tables to make way for the coffee, Paul Sprygelly had witnessed the exchange. He'd seen similar exchanges in the town many times before. On several occasions, before his arrest, his Uncle Denzel had even suggested Paul become a special club member himself.

   Things hadn't worked out quite so well for Uncle Denzel. It had been virtually impossible for anyone in the town to learn what had occurred.
The rumours had suggested that Uncle Denzel had been arrested along with the strange bloke from Emmety Villa. No one knew why though. It had been suggested it was something to do with the underwear thefts in the town, but despite the absence of Denzel and Maurice, laundry was still disappearing from lines in some areas. It was also being reported that a similar thing was happening in Polperro, four miles away. Perhaps there was a link?

Paul had long conversations with his girlfriend Lisa, speculating. Paul had asked Lisa if her mum or cousin WPC Veryan, had volunteered anything, but they had both been as discreet as they usually were and simply said "It's confidential and I can't discuss it".
The local paper hadn't published anything about it either, not even a court report. All that anyone knew with certainty was that Denzel Sprygelly was due for release from a six- month prison sentence on Friday, just one week away.

Lisa's mum was police Sargent Lowenna Bolitho, which made Paul and Lisa distant cousins. That didn't trouble anyone in their small community. So many people were related by marriage that the catchphrase for the town was "We're all cousins here!"

Paul brought himself back to the present. He knew in the next hour he'd serve another twenty pots of coffee and get through another half-box of the specially wrapped biscuits. He knew the visitors would take every opportunity to fill their pockets and handbags with anything they thought was free. He made a mental note to order extra toilet rolls when he did the housekeeping purchase later. It was amazing that almost every room seemed to run out every day when the coaches brought their weekly deliveries of retiree's.

It was going to be a busier than usual day for the upcoming Easter weekend. The employment compliance officer was visiting to inspect the books. Paul mused on this. Mark Wray, the compliance officer, had been looking at all of Uncle Denzel's businesses over the last few months. Paul remembered Mark from when he'd lived in the town several years before. He was a popular man, and even more popular now that people were being paid a minimum wage and being issued with contracts. Uncle Denzel had been a big fish, and like several others in the town, had paid appalling low wages. That was changing rapidly now.

Uncle Denzel had owned a majority share in the hotel before his arrest. Apparently, he had sold his interest to cover some legal fees.
Everyone on the staff felt much happier knowing that Uncle Denzel couldn't pressurise them anymore.

Paul sincerely hoped that he wouldn't be asked to collect Uncle Denzel from Dartmoor prison on Friday.

Outside a bar on the other side of the river, Cowboy and his friend Uncle Keith waited as bolts were drawn back on the inside and the doors were finally opened.

"Come on Robbie" Cowboy demanded "It's almost 10'oclock, I'm dying of thirst out here."

Robbie, one of Denzel's cousins, fitted the hook on the back of the door to stop it swinging and smiled at Cowboy. "You do know we're not supposed to serve you until eleven O'clock? It's supposed to be breakfast and coffee's only".

"Yeah, yeah Robbie, look, I just want a hair of the dog. You tell me every day. Have a rum yourself by any chance?"

Robbie smiled. They went through this routine every morning. Recently Uncle Keith had been coming every morning too. Clearly, he and Cowboy were planning something. Knowing Cowboy, probably something not entirely legal.

Robbie beckoned them in and decided not to notice that Uncle Keith was wearing bright blue nail varnish today. He usually wore green.

Around the town, the pace of life was speeding up as businesses and residents prepared themselves for the first busy weekend of the year.

In the small supermarket, Jimmy was doing his best to keep the shelves filled with bread and milk and eggs. Easter was always a juggle. Some people didn't seem to understand that two Bank Holidays and a Sunday meant that there was a huge influx of people into the town, and hence significantly increased demand.

Jimmy, left in charge of the ordering when his new manager realised that he just didn't have the knowledge or experience, also had to juggle with the additional problem of how to warehouse what would be needed in what was basically a glorified shed. Jimmy was sweating. He wished his former colleague Mike would come back. Mike had his own shop now though, he was finally free of the company, and loving it. As he piled swiss rolls onto the fittings, Jimmy fantasised about handing in his notice.

Jimmy's manager, Dermot, was keeping his head down in the office pretending to be engaged with something vitally important. He hadn't got his diploma in business studies just so he could work. All the staff knew how to run the shop better than he ever could anyway. It was for the best, he reasoned, that he just stayed out of their way and let them get on with it. He still got paid, whether he sat in the office or not.
When he'd had his initiation training, Jeremy, his coaching manager, had suggested that Dermot work alongside his staff. "Show them how you want it done." he'd said, "Set the standard." Dermot had done his best, but at the end of the second day, he had an aching back and paper cuts from the cardboard. He had abraded the skin between his thumb and forefingers tugging off cellophane wrapping, and twice while he'd been kneeling to fill the bottom shelves, he'd been bashed in the head with shopping baskets. What made things even more embarrassing was that the only section

he'd managed to fill was the toilet paper. Afterwards, Jimmy had rearranged it all. Jimmy explained there was a company merchandising shelf-plan. Dermot had no idea what this was.

Dermot looked at the clock and wondered if it was too early to go out for his lunch.
Lunch was going to consist mostly of lager.

Dermot had taken a ninety-minute lunch break every day since his arrival a few weeks earlier. He'd generally make some comment about not taking his tea breaks. Joyce on the checkout, who had seen many managers come and go during her forty years there, knew that Dermot didn't need a tea break. He already had the other staff members fetching him tea and coffee on their breaks. Joyce was biding her time to see how things worked out. The minute Dermot began thinking he could interfere with the running of the shop; she would begin her usual routine of tricks to get him to leave.
"Next customer please" Joyce called out cheerfully.
She looked up to see Monkey standing in front of her clutching a loaf and a newspaper which he unloaded awkwardly onto the counter. Joyce noticed the bulge under his left arm but as she hadn't seen anything on the CCTV screen. She knew she wasn't allowed to say anything. It was probably another leg of lamb. Joyce politely served Monkey without confrontation and bid him goodbye. She missed the old days when she'd been allowed to challenge shop lifters, or even chase them sometimes.

Virtually everyone in the town had a nickname, whether they knew it or not was another matter.

"Next customer please." Joyce called. Mr and Mrs Walrus stepped forward. They probably didn't know their nicknames.
Joyce took in the contents of their basket in a glance. That's a lot of cake she thought quietly to herself.

The peaceful atmosphere was shattered by a loud shout of "What do you mean there's no lime jelly?"
Someone else was having a drama. Poor Jimmy, it was going to be another testing weekend for all of them. Most of the valued visitors hadn't begun to arrive yet. Joyce hoped Jimmy had plenty of Prozac or whatever it was he took to keep himself so cheerful.

On the beach, Tony maneuvered the tractor skilfully to push another bucket-load of rancid seaweed into a position where the tide would carry it back out to sea.

Few people understood what an art there was to clean the beach. Tony, after years of practice, had become quite adept. Most of the casual onlookers seemed to think all the effort was purely for the aesthetic. Tony knew that the rotting weed harboured E Coli and other nasty bacteria. The last thing the town needed was a reputation for stomach upsets. On the other hand, he pondered as he rolled the tractor along the beach for another scoop, if people could use the public toilets and survive, the seaweed was probably inconsequential. Either way, he knew that for just a few minutes, once he'd finished raking and scooping, the beach would look as tidy as a Japanese garden.

From the cab of the tractor, Tony glanced at the barely lapping water and the bright white yacht which had been anchored just a little way offshore since the night before. There were two kayaks paddling toward the yacht. Ordinarily, Tony would have thought nothing of them, but to his sharp eyes, the inept kayakers appeared to be Cowboy and Uncle Keith.
Tony's first thought was to wonder where on earth the pair had gotten their wetsuits, they looked like something from a 1950's war film.
He turned his attention back to the job in hand. At least Uncle Keith wasn't flashing again.
Tony allowed himself to chuckle. Uncle Keith had attempted to flash at his mother last week. Keith had underestimated just how sprightly Tony's mother was, and she'd managed to club him with her walking stick at least a dozen times before a pair of well-meaning cliff path

walkers had come along and rescued the pervert.

After the incident, Tony had asked his mother why everyone called the ridiculous flasher Uncle Keith. She'd explained that at one time he'd had a big family in the town. Most of them had moved away in an attempt to disassociate themselves from him. Most had left after he'd appeared in a series of desperate attempts to compete in 'Stars in their eyes'.

One of the problems was that Uncle Keith kept telling people he'd won, which he hadn't. He also embraced the roles a bit too enthusiastically. He'd been Cliff Richard for a whole year and had kept insisting he was addressed as Sir Cliff. He was Elaine Paige the next year, and the year after that, he'd really upset people when he'd taken on the identity of Margaret Thatcher for 12 months.
No one wanted to talk about that.
The only other Keith in the town at the time had been Keith Harris, the butcher, or Keith the meat as he was generally known. Uncle Keith had just stuck.

Tony wasn't the only one watching. From the coastguard station at Hannafore, three pairs of curious eyes were fixed to binoculars watching the kayaks as they paddled seaward. There were two old codgers wearing gear which looked like it had come from the antiques roadshow. They'd probably just bought the kayaks and were going for an exploratory paddle. The coastguard team had decided to watch them just in case they got into difficulties.

The team had already checked the yachts registration. She was registered in Portugal, but marine logs had shown that she'd recently been visiting Dutch waters. Anything which had come from the Netherlands was always worth a look. There was nothing suspicious about this one though, and her logs matched her planned itinerary.

An alarm sounded in the coastguard station and Gary, the station master, put down his binoculars and reached for the radio to answer the incoming call. Apparently, there had been a sighting from a fishing boat of a cluster of four shipping containers which were floating in the sea just off Polperro. These were probably the ones full of Polish vodka which had been bound for Southampton. They'd washed off the deck of a container ship as she'd worked her way up the Cornish coast. The coastguard weren't the only ones looking for them.

Gary knew he'd need both his other team members for this, not to mention police and air support. The kayakers would have to depend on themselves now. His team had an emergency to deal with.

In the calm waters of the Bay, Cowboy and Uncle Keith had finally reached the yacht. They paddled around the hull until they were out of sight of the immediate shoreline. They had a collection to make. If this went well, it would be the first of many.
Cowboy and Uncle Keith were excited.

Donald and Sylvia were exploring, as were most of the rest of their group. It had been 5 years since they'd last visited and they reminisced as they walked along the quay. Donald pointed at the amusement arcade as they approached the bridge.

"I remember that place, it's in that photograph of our Rodney and Ella, the Blue something wasn't it?"

Sylvia remembered only too well. She and her family had been visiting Looe since the 1960's. As a teenager she'd hoped to get a job as a dancer in the building Donald was indicating. It had been a cinema, she remembered, and then a proper night club.

"Shark Donald, it was called the Blue Shark Club"

"Wasn't that the place with those exotic dancers?" Donald asked knowing full well it had been.

He'd been coming to Looe for years with his family too, it was how he and Sylvia had met. Too young to get into the club then, Donald had spent hours outside peering through a gap in the curtains trying to get a glimpse of 'Sarah and her snake'. Acts like that were considered quite modern and popular back then, sophisticated even. For a lad from Solihull, Sarah and her snake had been an education, especially once he learned she used to smoke outside the back doors between turns.

Sylvia enjoyed her memories of the place in silence too. The doormen always used to let the pretty girls in, whether they were old enough or not. Sylvia would spend hours on the dancefloor whenever her parents made their regular visits to their favourite campsite just on the edge of the town. She could wiggle like a lemur in those days. Nowadays the only time she wiggled was when she thought her hip was going to give way.

As they crossed the bridge, a large white Space Explorer type vehicle stopped in the middle of the road in the centre of the bridge. Clearly it was obstructing the rest of the traffic, but the driver had decided he wanted to have a good look at the view. What did it matter to him if other people were trying to get somewhere? He was on holiday.

A considerable queue had built up and Donald and Sylvia had reached the other end of the bridge before any of the other drivers began to impatiently beep their horns. Coming from the other direction was a man in a large camper van. He was attempting to read a map at as he steered his home for the next two months onto the bridge.

The taxi behind him held back waiting for the inevitable. Fortunately, the pavements were empty. The only pedestrian on the bridge was Police sergeant Lowenna Bolitho, and she had seen all too clearly what was occurring with both drivers.
Raymond, the taxi driver, one of Denzel's cousins, was rewarded with a satisfying crunch as camper van idiot collided with space explorer idiot.
Lowenna stepped in immediately to clear the blockage. She instructed both vehicles to drive into the police station car park and wait for her. The drivers meekly did as they were instructed.

Donald and Sylvia began the long process of walking around all the gift shops and looking at things they had no intention of buying. It was almost 12.30 now, and they had arranged to meet their new friends in the cosy little pub right in the heart of the town, the one with the coal fire. It was a bright sunny day, but the air was cool and most of the pedestrians still wore coats and hats.

Donald reasoned he could stand a few of these tedious gift shop circuits, just as long as he could also get at least four pints inside him while sitting in front of a warm fire. Sylvia seemed to enjoy looking, and so dutiful Donald went along with it nodding and smiling at the appropriate times.

Sylvia was pretending to be interested in souvenirs. She reasoned she could stand a few of these tedious gift shop circuits, just as long as she could also get at least four gin and tonics inside her while sitting in front of a warm fire. Donald seemed to enjoy looking, and so dutiful Sylvia went along with it nodding and smiling at the appropriate times.

Just occasionally, they would make a note of a tacky resin fridge magnet or a commemorative china thimble for one of their friends, it was a game they played.

'We've been on holiday more than you.' It ought to have been called. Neighbours and friends from the allotments and bingo would all receive something commemorative every time one of the group went away. Whenever there was a gathering at each other's houses, as often happened, the players could sit and proclaim how much they'd contributed to the overloaded fridges and freezers. "Oh look Beryl, that's that funny little hedgehog I bought you in Salisbury that time." And "Hahaha Barry, I see you've still got that little burned out car magnet I got you in St Austell."

Secretly, most of them hated the bloody awful magnets, but everyone was too polite to say anything, let alone fail to display one. Consequently, the competition had evolved to a point where the competitors sought out only the most hideous of offerings.

Looe certainly had plenty to offer fridge magnet enthusiasts. There were nasty resin impressions of the town bridge and the Banjo pier, there were piskies with fibre beards and springy legs, there were lighthouses and crabs and lobsters and ice creams all rendered in the finest quality plastics. It was an environmental catastrophe, and people couldn't get enough of them, Donald and Sylvia included. Their fridge magnet budget for this trip was thirty pounds, and they were going to have no trouble at all in spending it. But not today, not until they'd been everywhere.

In Skegness last summer they'd seen some twinkling unicorn head magnets, although what unicorns had to do with Skegness is anyone's guess. Sylvia had purchased four for £1.99 each. A little further along the seafront, they'd found the same unicorns but on offer at 4 for the price of 3.
Taking the original purchase back to the first shop had exploded into a big drama. Donald had been embarrassed and urged Sylvia to just accept what had happened. Sylvia, always careful with money, had stood her ground. The poor beleaguered shopkeeper had refunded her and given her an extra magnet just to get her out of his shop.

Sylvia was an avid collector of teddy bears; she noted the prices as they progressed towards the seafront. Donald was busy making a note of the price of fudge everywhere. Before they went home, Sylvia and Donald would be in possession of some of the best bargains Looe had to offer.

As they progressed down the street, Sylvia remembered the Guildhall Market. She'd brought some fabulous underwear there in the past. She decided to give Donald a holiday treat.

Pointing at the café next door she said "Why don't you get us some tea Donald? I just want to pop in here and get a few postcards"

Donald was delighted, he'd spotted a pharmacy just over the road and he'd heard it was possible to buy Viagra over the counter now. While Sylvia was in the market, he'd discreetly pop over the road and ask. If he could get some here. If he could, he wouldn't need any more £20 for 2 deals from druggie Kevin at the snooker club. Hotel rooms had a certain effect on Sylvia, and he needed to be ready. Donald mentally checked his list. He was going to need ibuprofen gel, two good tubular knee supports, a good dose of zinc supplements and of course, the all-important little blue pills.

Things had been slowing down in the intimacy department recently, but Donald was determined to show Sylvia he was just as virile as he'd ever been
Sylvia was in for a holiday surprise.

Alan Higginbottom watched as the estate agent's boardman hammered a stake into the soft turf at the front of Emmety Villa.

There had been a lot of changes recently, and soon there would be new people to get used to. Alan fervently hoped the vacant flats would attract residents rather than owners who wanted to rent them out as holiday lets. Better still, the flats would remain unsold and vacant.

Both the top flat, laughingly called the penthouse, and the ground floor holiday let, had been put on the market at the end of the previous summer. Both sets of owners had been having far too many problems while letting them out. Alan now had some insights as to why.

The other ground floor flat had been emptied and put on the market when the owner had been sent to prison a few months previously. Alan had given evidence in court. Maurice John Thomas as he was addressed in court, had pleaded guilty to multiple counts of theft. There were also some references to incidents of fraud in Bristol.

Maurice would be staying in accommodation with an exceedingly small window for the foreseeable future. Outside the court, a man identifying himself as a special club member by his initial handshake, had instructed Alan that he wasn't to discuss any part of the trial. Alan had simply shaken the offered hand without returning the identifying gesture. Alan didn't want anything to do with the special club.

Alan wondered if his cousin, Denzel, would try to persuade him to join the special club again when he got out of prison. Denzel had been tried on different charges at the same court. Alan had even been in the building when Cousin Denzel and Maurice had been arrested. He shuddered and then remembered one of the good things which had come out of the incident, now he had a wizard's outfit.

Eileen had been very understanding. She'd returned from her sisters on the day of all the police activity, to find a clearly distressed Alan hiding beneath the kitchen table. He was wearing the wizard outfit and he was clearly under the influence of something hallucinogenic. Eileen realised that this must have been as a result of Alan's initiation into the Special club the night before. She'd helped him to bed agreeing that he could keep the star covered robe and pointy hat. Later, when he was lucid, he'd tried to remember what had happened, but his memory was clouded after the first half hour of the evening.
They had agreed never to discuss it again, and that he could wear the purple robe and hat inside the flat, but never beyond those walls. Alan had other ideas about that, and they had gone out as Wizard and Witch on New Year's Eve.
Eileen seemed to quite like his outfit now and would sometimes cuddle up to him on the sofa and whisper "Do you want to show me your magic wand?"
He turned his thoughts back to the board-man. What if he didn't like the look of whoever came to view? He'd have to think of ways to put them off. Alan had been acting as unofficial caretaker at Emmety Villa since the end of the previous summer, and he had keys for all the apartments now. He'd have to get creative.

The police had taken away more than 20 black bags full of lingerie and rubber-wear from Maurice's place. It had been impossible to separate all that had been legitimately purchased, from the items Maurice had stolen from washing lines.

Afterwards, Maurice's estranged wife had asked Alan to help dispose of the remainder of the contents of the apartment. Satisfied that her husband was in prison, Doris was happy to accept the proceeds of the sale of the flat. She wanted nothing from the contents except for a few photographs.

Alan and Eileen had put on thick rubber gloves and had boxed up everything domestic that could be reused and sent it off to a local charity. They'd joked as they worked. Maurice would have probably approved of the rubber gloves.
This still left a selection of personal items though, and Alan and Eileen had been a little taken aback by some of the more intimate items. Between them they had made sure the boxes were thoroughly taped up before taking them to the tip.

The only things Alan had kept were a bunch of keys which turned out to fit assorted locks in the building, and a hardback notebook with the words 'Anti-Emmet-Ideas' written on the front in biro. Alan and Eileen had been fascinated at the workings of their former neighbours' peculiar mind. The front had an assortment of words and schemes which it looked as if Maurice had been putting into place whenever visitors arrived. The back half contained a series of notes of addresses, names and some personal notes on the people who lived there.

'Number 48 Trenant Road, Tom & Dora Willitt, Wash day, Mondays mixed, boring.
Number 67 Trenant Road, Brian Collins, Wash day Fridays, some frillies, some rubber. Hangs up inside shed'

Number 8 Pendennis, Vera Barker, wash day Saturday………Lovely!

The notes went on to the end of the book.
The most disturbing thing was that Alan and Eileen either knew or were related to most of the people who were named. Eileen was particularly distressed to learn that the mayor, who was single now, had quite a substantial collection of red ladies' lingerie.
"Oh no! Not Uncle Alfred as well." she'd exclaimed.
Alan was interested to see if there was any more detail about Vera. She was his cousin, but then, so was Eileen. Alan had always fancied Vera.

Eileen had dropped the book into one of the boxes that was destined for the tip, but Alan had retrieved it. It was in his shed now, tucked away in the folder with all the instruction booklets he insisted on keeping. Alan had been studying it.

Alan had also been watching a series of tutorials on witchcraft on YouTube. He had the outfit, now he'd decided, he wanted to be a proper wizard. Eileen had thought he was just being silly. She was glad he'd found a new interest, especially after the disappointment following his attempt to join the special club. Men needed their toys and games and fun things, as did their wives. Eileen had one or two ideas about how to entertain herself too, and she had to be honest, she'd always rather liked the idea of becoming a witch.

Alan decided to wait and see who arrived with the estate agent before he adopted any of Maurice's methods. He could always ask Cousin Lowenna to check up on people.

She wouldn't be able to tell him very much, but after the Maurice incident, as it was now referred to, any information at all would be helpful in making an assessment.

Donald sat at a table inside the café watching one of the staff members cleaning tables. His trip to the pharmacy had been successful and he now had four little blue tablets in his inside jacket pocket. They had only cost £38. Donald was pleased. Druggie Kev could keep his high-priced merchandise, except for the Lebanese slate of course. Donald and Eileen were children of the 60's, there were some things they'd never give up.
Donald watched the young waitress clean a seagull strike from the last of the outside tables, and then followed her in with his eyes. Once she was back behind the counter, she began cleaning the cake cabinet with the same cloth. Donald was relieved he'd only ordered tea.

Sylvia joined him after just a few moments. In her younger days, the items she'd just purchased would have been suitable for National Service use. They were full and robust. At her age, Sylvia liked full and robust. She expected Donald would like them too.
Sylvia had something else on her mind and as Donald was clearly in a particularly good mood, she decided now was a good time to mention it.
"You know we always said we'd retire here?"
Donald guessed what was coming next.
"You'd like to look at the estate agents?"
Sylvia beamed at him.
"Yes, I would love. We've still got an hour before we're due to meet Norman and Marjorie. Why don't we go and have a quick look in that one by the supermarket?"
Donald nodded to indicate his agreement. He would happily move to Cornwall if they found somewhere suitable. His only possible concern was how long it would take him to find a new dealer. Probably not long in this town, he'd been noticing wafts of marijuana smoke ever

since they'd been walking through the High Street.
"I must just nip to the loo first love" he answered.
This would be his fifth visit since they'd crossed the bridge, once for every shop they'd been in. Sylvia nodded back at him. This would be her fourth.
"Me too, I'll see you over there. Did I mention you're looking very handsome today?"
"And you're looking gorgeous" Donald replied and leant across the table to give her a quick kiss.

The waitress with the grubby dishcloth, one of Denzel's nieces, averted her eyes as quickly as she could. She had to deal with some unpleasant things in her job, but that was absolutely disgusting. She felt sick.

A few minutes later they met on the pavement and looked at some of the properties on offer in the window. There were some beautiful houses, but they were a long way outside of Donald and Sylvia's price range. Inside the window, a young woman in a smart suit mounted a new set of details.
'Luxury apartments close to town centre' read the headline. The brief details showed three flats in the same building, and at a price Donald and Sylvia could afford.
"Well bugger me!" Donald exclaimed.
A complete stranger chipped in as he walked past.
"Not in the street mate, you have to go to the cruising beach if that's what you're looking for"
The passer-by laughed at his own joke and continued on his way.
For a second, the couple were speechless. Sylvia recovered first.
"What did he mean? And what were you referring to?"
Donald jerked his head towards the window.

"Look who's inside."
Sylvia peered through the glass and saw the distinct figures of Norman and Marjorie already sitting down and being shown a portfolio of properties.
"Well fancy that." she responded "I wonder if they've found anything interesting? Shall we go in?"
Donald moved towards the door and as he held it open for his beloved, gave her one of his best smiles.
"If we can find the right place, I reckon we could be very happy here"
As they stepped inside and the door swung closed, they completely missed the latest drama to unfold in the street behind them.

Next to the Guildhall on the other side of the road, a busker had been playing for about an hour. The customers and staff in the café had enjoyed his performance as much as the passers-by. The Barbers had been enjoying it too, and so had the people using the offices on the higher floors of the estate agents building. The only person who wasn't enjoying it apparently, was Patrick the picture framer. Patrick had been deputy mayor once about 25 years ago. Patrick considered himself one of the town's most important people.
Full of self-importance and bluster, Patrick had waddled over the road and waved a pudgy finger at the musician, telling him he wasn't allowed to be playing in that area.

The busker it transpired, as was often the case, knew the law a lot better than his challenger, and was now showing up Patrick for the pompous, preposterous little twerp he really was.
Patrick, too stupid to know when to walk away, had begun to suggest he would call the police. The busker had

welcomed this and offered to phone them himself.
By now, Patrick was becoming more and more agitated, and his behaviour was becoming increasingly hostile and abusive.

A crowd was gathering. As Patrick became more abusive, they booed and hissed. As the busker politely held his ground and tried to calm the righteous former deputy mayor, the crowd applauded him.
The exchange had been running for 15 minutes now. The barbers had stopped cutting hair and had come out to join the growing body of witnesses.
"I was deputy mayor here once and I know all the local bylaws." Patrick kept repeating. The crowd booed.
"That's great," the busker countered "you'll know you have no right to prevent me going about my lawful business in a public area then." The crowd gave a small cheer.

Patrick was losing face and finally lost control altogether. He lunged forward attempting to grab the guitar. As he stepped forward, he tripped on the curb and hurtled into the low wall which separated the Rose garden from the pavement. The crowd gasped and then cheered, louder this time. Patrick picked himself up. There were fires in his eyes.
He pulled back his right arm intending to take a swing at the irritating affable musician and found himself grasped firmly around his chest and lifted off the ground.
The crowd cheered as Sargent Lowenna turned an abrupt 180 degrees and carried Patrick towards the police car he'd failed to notice arriving.
Patrick had caused trouble in the town before and Lowenna had an extremely low tolerance for bullies. She growled in his ear just loud enough for him to hear "Hush

up now Patrick, you wouldn't want to hurt yourself, would you?"

Patrick remembered his last encounter with the Sargent. He'd been spying on his neighbours through their kitchen window. The neighbours happened to be Lowenna's son and his wife.
Lowenna had come up quietly behind him and picked him up in a bear hug that time too. Then, accidently, she'd said, she had dropped him down a flight of 11 concrete steps. Patrick was suddenly noticeably quiet and very cooperative.

Lowenna handcuffed Patrick and instructed him to sit quietly in the back of the car before having a quick word with the busker. The cheerful guitarist said he didn't want to press charges of harassment, but it would be great if the idiot could be inconvenienced. Lowenna approved of this method, convictions were difficult even with overwhelming evidence. She'd keep Patrick in a cell for a few hours and then send him to Launceston thirty miles to the north. That way, Patrick would be released late at night when there were no buses or taxis available. It was a long, gruelling walk from Launceston back to Looe.

As Lowenna drove away, the busker played "I fought the law" but changed the words to "He fought the law". The crowd loved it.

Cowboy and Uncle Keith were exhausted. They hadn't considered just how difficult it would be to paddle back to the harbour against an outgoing tide. At last, they had made it to the slipway, and now, with a great deal of puffing and panting, they dragged the borrowed kayaks out of the water.

"After all that hassle, we didn't need these bleedin flippers at all" Cowboy moaned.
Groaning all the way, they carried the kayaks back to the storage rack by the seafront fountain, feet flapping as they walked.
Luckily, while they'd been on the water, the real owners hadn't come along to discover the absence. Cowboy had dumped the padlocks and chains in the river. He'd gone to the seafront with bolt cutters under cover of darkness the night before. He probably could have borrowed them anyway, but it wasn't in his nature to ask.

Cowboy's girlfriend owned a guest house on the quayside. She wasn't at home this week, and so Cowboy and Uncle Keith had changed into the wetsuits there after they'd left the pub.
They flapped noisily back there now. Each of them with a small, well-sealed plastic bag of pills tucked into the crotches of their antique wetsuits.

"Phew" gasped Uncle Keith as he closed the front door behind him. He unzipped the side of his suit and rummaged between his legs.
"So, what exactly are they then?" Keith continued to rummage.

Cowboy always operated strictly on a need-to-know basis.

He sat on the bottom of the stairs and tugged off his flippers.
"The Dutchman said the blue ones were happy pills and the others would keep you up all night, I think he means they're some sort of amphetamine. It might have been the other way round" Cowboy began to walk up the stairs.
"I'm going to use the shower; I stink from this flippin outfit. I'll be back in a few minutes and then you can use it. Pour us a vodka and we can have a proper look once we're dressed"

Keith, flippers still firmly on his feet, began to flap and flop his way towards the kitchen.
"Have you got any lager?" he called after Cowboy. Cowboy didn't answer, so Keith opened the fridge and took out a fresh can. "Ah lovely." he said to himself. He sat at the table and examined the bag. The bags, they'd been told on the yacht, contained 50 pills each. If they were happy with them, the yacht would be back with more. These looked as if they were blue and diamond shaped. Keith was hoping that he and Cowboy were going to try them, after all, if he were going to be selling happy pills in the pubs locally, he'd need to know what they did.
It was a long time since his acid days, but unlike the remainder of his contemporaries, Uncle Keith hadn't realised he was getting older. He liked to drink, and if he could get anything stronger, he liked that too. It didn't seem to bother him at all that most of the people he knew thought he was a bit of a strange one. The words they frequently used were 'Bit of a twat', but most people were too polite to tell him to his face.
The song 'The oldest swinger in town' could have been written especially for him and his mate, Cowboy.

Uncle Keith had to buy his clothes from the retro shop in Plymouth now, anything else just looked wrong. At weekends, if he managed to get past the doormen at the local disco, in his addled mind, he was convinced he was as good as John Travolta, maybe even better.

He felt most at home when he joined the coach loads of visitors in the Looe River View Hotel. It was Cabaret night on Fridays, and Uncle Keith would strut his funky stuff all over the dancefloor. Now he thought about it, Cabaret was tomorrow. Perhaps he could sell a few pills there?

His revery was interrupted by the reappearance of Cowboy. The wetsuit was gone, and he was dressed in his best denims.

Uncle Keith flopped away to the bathroom to take his turn. He was sad to have to take the moist rubber away from his skin, it felt nice. Perhaps he could put it back on later.

A few hundred yards from where Cowboy and Uncle Keith were examining their new imports, Noman brought another tray of drinks to the table beside the fireplace. Spread out were the particulars for several properties. The ones for the apartments both couples liked, were being held by Sylvia now.

Both couples liked the look of the ground floor flats. The steps at the front didn't trouble them, and the garden looked well cared for. They all liked the idea it was communal as that meant presumably, everyone in the building helped to maintain it.
It was just a short walk to the town, and the agent had said that it was in a quiet part. The agent didn't live in Looe and in reality, had no idea of the noise which regularly bombarded Emmety Villa.

"Just think," Marjorie said, "We could be neighbours." and then quickly asked "Which one do you prefer?" Marjorie had already decided which one she liked better, and as far as she was concerned, she and Norman had been in the estate agents first. They were going to view all three available apartments in the morning.

Donald was a little distracted by a strange looking trio who were laughing loudly at the bar. They looked different from what he was used to, but they were clearly enjoying themselves and seemed good humoured. If these were another sample of the locals, he was even more certain he'd like to live here. The three looked as if they were all in their 50's. The youngest one was conventional with a loose grandad shirt and short haircut. The taller one looked startlingly like a native American and had somehow managed to dress the part, and yet look completely normal

in this setting. The other one had a full Buffalo Bill set of whiskers and was wearing an anti-Nazi league tee shirt. They were clearly old friends. Cider was being consumed steadily and the laughter was flowing as the conversation ebbed and flowed. Evidently two of them were playing in a band the following night. The younger chap was asking a question,
"Why on earth did you call it the Far Canal Denis?" he was asking.
Donald had seen the name written on a chalk bord outside as his party had come in. The native American leaned towards his friend and answered, "Because that's what you're ginna say win you hear us play Batfink, int it Wynn?" he looked at Buffalo Bill and grinned, the trio laughed uproariously.
Batfink, Denis and Wynn as they'd now been identified, ordered another round.
Donald wondered if he'd be allowed to stay in the pub. They were clearly enjoying themselves he thought, he'd love to join them.

He brought his attention back to the discussion at his own table. "Did you book a viewing?" Norman was asking "We're booked in to see all three apartments at 10.30." and then added, "I do hope it's one of the ladies we spoke to today and not some spotty little twerp in a shiny Tesco fifty quid three-piece suit".

Donald laughed, he recognised the type immediately. "Oh yes" he agreed jovially, "They're like that around our way too, just left school and they're all so intelligent and bursting with life experience, even though they still live with their mums."
Norman nodded in agreement "I definitely prefer the older ones, at least they know what they're talking about." He

snorted and continued, "As for the younger one, little shits most of them; condescending, patronising, sanctimonious" Marjorie chipped in, "That's right darling, and that's your job, isn't it?" she winked.
Clearly the gins and beers were doing their job, the four pensioners were laughing as loudly as the trio at the bar now.

Sylvia waited until the laughter had subsided before saying, "We were booked in to view at 11.30. Would you mind if we came around with you though? It would save whoever it is having to take us all around twice."
"Of course we wouldn't mind would we Donald? We might as well make a foursome." Both men raised their eyebrows in a gesture worthy of a Benny Hill gag as Marjorie began to blush and then burst at laughing.

As the laughter diminished, the trio at the bar were getting ready to leave. "Thank you so much for your hostility" Denis announced as he waved to the room in general, burst out laughing, and made his way to the door.
The barman laughed, "You three go steady", he called after them, "and remember…....", as if pre-scripted Batfink, Wynn and Denis looked back at the bar and as one voice finished for him," Moderation". As the door closed, their laughter followed them down the street.

Dermot was leaving the supermarket just as local celebrity Rachael De'Sprygelly was entering. She was clearly disappointed when people failed to recognise her. Rachael presented the weather reports on a local television station and in her mind, she was as famous as Debbie Harry.

She had only just been allowed back inside the supermarket following a twelve-month ban. She knew she was going to repeat what she'd done before, even if it got her into trouble again. Rachael just couldn't help herself.

She would pick up a bottle of fizz and tub of cream and put them in her basket. Next, she would cram a packet of meringues and a packet of strawberries into her handbag. Then she would attempt to exit the shop having only paid for two of the four items. No one understood why she did this, she didn't understand it herself, it was just some sort of weird Pavlovian response.

Jimmy saw Rachael coming in, but to be honest, she was hard to miss. She was just under five feet tall, but she had a bust that was hard to navigate around the narrower areas of the shop. It didn't matter to Jimmy that her eyes were at different heights on her face, or that she wore so much make up that she looked like the local kids had practised face painting on her, Jimmy adored her. Of all the oddbods that ever came to Looe, she was his favourite. Jimmy realised she couldn't help herself with the meringue thing, although of course, she did help herself. If Jimmy had been Mars, then Rachael was his Venus. He hurried to the till on the pretence of giving Joyce her break. He needed to be in place for the longest possible window of conversation. Rachael smiled up the aisle at Jimmy. She knew he liked her, and she certainly liked him. He reminded her of her favourite Start trek character. For a moment, she wondered if he knew anything about Oo-mox. Rachael had some experience of men, but now, she was saving herself for the man who she'd give her heart to. If that happened to be Jimmy, she was going to ride him like a Harley. She felt herself flush as she thought about the discount Jimmy would be able to get on meringues.

Joyce spotted her cousin coming up the first aisle, no wonder Jimmy had rushed to the till. She smiled inwardly and hoped that the two would get past the pussy footing stage and finally manage to arrange to go out on a date. In a town where so many people were related, Jimmy was a catch. He might not have been considered quite that anywhere else she thought, what with all his funny little ways, but he was a happy soul, and reliable, and most important of all, he wasn't from the Looe gene-pool.

Joyce had been coaching Jimmy for weeks "Ask her questions about herself, be funny, get her to understand you don't have any cousins here"
Joyce had even been teaching Jimmy how to tell jokes, the problem was that most of Joyce's jokes were unrepeatable on the shop floor. Jimmy would go scarlet at the mention of anything in the least rude. Joyce knew jokes that would have made the devil himself blush.

Rachael crammed a crispy eight pack of nests into her bag alongside the strawberries and maneuvered herself into position to approach the till.
Jimmy finished serving 'Blend Brian'. He'd been named that by the landlady of the towns much lamented Double-Decker bars. The full first part was Bell-end, but in Cornish fashion it had been shortened. Brian assumed, wrongly, that the 'Blend' part came from when he used to serve coffees in The Petrie Dish café. Those who knew the truth would just smile inwardly. Most people, Brian included, never realised.
As Brian moved away, Rachael stepped forward.
Jimmy did his best to make eye contact, but this was often a challenge when it came to Rachael. He tried to focus on her

nose, but her blouse was bursting and what was on display was totally disempowering so he failed miserably.

They began their usual routine.
"Hi Jimmy"
"Hi Rachael"
"You alright?"
"Yes thanks, you?"
   Jimmy ignored Rachael's obviously full handbag as he passed the Prosecco and cream across the scanner.

"That's six pounds and forty-eight pence please" he smiled brightly.
Rachael was already holding her bank card towards the pay-point terminal. "I'm not working tomorrow Jimmy, are you doing anything in the afternoon? "

Jimmy was so surprised by the question that for a few seconds he just moved his mouth soundlessly.
Rachael looked puzzled, then again, with eyes like hers, that was an almost permeant expression. Jimmy collected himself.
"Actually, I'm going to look at a flat tomorrow afternoon. What did you have in mind?" His heart was pounding now, and he could feel himself beginning to perspire.
"I wondered if you'd like to come and have a drink with me?" Jimmy took an involuntary step back. Rachael didn't seem to notice and continued. "Oh, are you buying it or renting, it sounds very exciting." Inside her head, cogs were whirring almost audibly.
"I'm opening the cabaret at the Looe River View tomorrow night; I'll be dressed up" she tilted her head and winked seductively "as the easter bunny" she finished.
Jimmy could feel himself becoming increasingly moist beneath his polyester shirt and he felt his face flush as a vision of Rachael dressed in rabbit ears flashed before his eyes.

"Erm, err, but yes, of course, I mean, great, erm….."
And just then Joyce reappeared, just in time to rescue him. "I'm not working tomorrow Jimmy, I can give you a lift" she turned to Rachael "What time shall I drop him off love?"
Rachael and Jimmy were about to go out on their first date.

In the police station, Lowenna put the phone down. The mayor was trying to rescue the traditional Good Friday parade. Usually, Lowenna would have to close the main road through the town to traffic for half an hour. The volunteer Jesus would carry his crucifix along to the beach. He would wear a mock crown of thorns and a sack-cloth robe. There would be a drummer and an escort of centurions who would poke him with their spears. They'd tried to stop the whipping part, as one of the former lord mayors had a bit of a thing for whips and had gotten rather carried away a few years previously. It wouldn't have been so bad but his 'centurions tunic' had ripped open revealing a studded patent leather onesie underneath, and the whip had been clearly made for use at a bondage party.
Last year's drummer hadn't quite managed an appropriate beat either. Everyone put that down to the fact that he usually played with a Samba group.

The mayor was having problems. The planned Jesus was away at a Buddhist retreat in Somerset having marked the wrong date on his calendar. Emergency Jesus had been involved in a bad accident involving a tube of 'no more nails' and was going to be 'stuck' in hospital for at least a couple of days while he was un-stuck. There had even been a third Jesus, Emergency reserve Jesus. Unfortunately, Good Friday coincided with the Elvis convention being held at one of the towns huge holiday parks and clearly, it was going to be a lot more fun to be Elvis than it was being Jesus, and so he'd dropped out.
The only person Lowenna could think of was her cousin Morley. He'd been Jesus a few times and he was rather good at it. Morley loved dressing up and he would always thoroughly immerse himself in the part. Morley had moved to Sheffield at the end of the last summer where he'd

opened a proper pasty shop. It would mean a long drive and an overnight stay, but Lowenna decided to give him a ring and ask him if he was free. It was unlikely he'd been selling many pasties in Sheffield on Chocolate Sunday after all.

As she took her phone from her pocket it beeped with a message from WPC Veryan. "It appears that Maurice had a rival, about a dozen people have lost underwear from their lines in the village in the last month, will fill you in when I get back"
Veryan was in Polperro. She'd gone to make enquiries about a box of KitKat's that had been stolen from a delivery left in front of the little newsagent. Whenever she went there, dozens of people would come forward to report all the latest goings on. Lowenna shook her head slowly, she really would like it if people rang her to report things, rather than store them all up. She re-read Veryan's message. Not another one. Catching and then prosecuting Maurice John Thomas had been a success. Sargent Lowenna hadn't thought for a moment that someone else might be filching panties too. Lowenna and Veryan both had plenty of cousins in the village. She'd have to arrange an evening outing.

Turning her mind back to the Easter parade, she began to dial Cousin Morley.
"Hi Morley, it's your cousin"
They made small talk before Lowenna could get to the point. Morley really did like to get into character, and today for some bizarre reason, he was Abraham Lincoln.
Lowenna went along with him until she got his agreement. It was with some relief that she terminated the call. Now it was time to call the Mayor back.

"Hello Colin, I have a Jesus for you"

"Oh wonderful, who is it?" the mayor sounded relieved. The Easter parade was an old if not ancient tradition in the town.
Lowenna explained.

"Cousin Morley said he'd drive down first thing in the morning. He can't stay until Sunday though; he has to open his shop on Saturday. He said he'll be happy to be Jesus, he'll just have to make sure he gets a good manicure this evening. You remember how he always used to like getting his nails done at Easter?"

There was a stifled guffaw from the other end of the phone.
Colin thanked his cousin heartily and hung up.

That afternoon the preparations for Easter continued. Beer was delivered, the number of pasties being baked increased tenfold. Bacon and eggs and ice cream were delivered by the trolly load to the multitude of cafes and food outlets. The posties struggled around the town delivering huge bundles of pointless promotional materials that the recipients would be too busy to read.

In the Looe River View Hotel, Donald planted himself firmly on the divan for an afternoon nap. In another room, Norman and Marjorie were doing the same thing. Sylvia had closed the bathroom door on Donald as she'd run herself a deep bath. The brochure had told them that there was Cabaret tomorrow, and that meant that this evening was her chance for a romantic night in.

In the bar of the Galleon, Cowboy and Uncle Keith were plotting how to infiltrate the Looe River View Hotel Cabaret the following evening. They could have just paid the £3 non-resident entry fee but sneaking in was far more in keeping with their characters.

In the police station Lowenna and Veryan discussed plans and duties for the busy weekend ahead.
In the supermarket, Jimmy was in a state of nervous hysteria. He was both excited and terrified at the prospect of his date the following day. He'd only ever kissed a girl once before, and Rachael clearly had plans for him, he could see it in her eye, the higher of the two.
Dermot had stumbled back into the shop and retreated into the office leaving a trail of lager fumes behind him.

At Emmety Villa, Alan was planning his evening too. It was cabaret night tomorrow which meant fancy dress in the Looe River View Hotel. Alan loved his wizard outfit, and he took every available opportunity to wear it. Eileen was going to be away overnight, so Alan had decided he was going to dress up, and then go out and mingle. He decided to ask his friend Ryan along. Ryan had one of the most interesting fancy dress costumes in the town. It had been especially made for him. His nickname was 'The salmon' although the origins of that particular nickname were long forgotten. Ryan, when bedecked in his splendour, was certainly one of the most impressive fish in the town. There were other fish of course, it was a popular choice in a seaside fishing town, but none could rival The Salmon, he had a unique way of moving.

In the Looe River View Hotel, other things were happening. Mark Wray was working his way through a list of employees and interviewing them. He compared their accounts with the records on file. Like most places in the town, it appeared that a lot of unpaid work was going on. Employees were being cheated of meal breaks and frequently working excessive hours. Few had contracts, and those who did had contracts that failed to recognise updates in employment law going back as far as 1948.
A new face was looking around the door, Mark beckoned the man in indicating the chair. He checked his list.

"Come in, have a seat. Would you like some tea?" He indicated the tea making set up at the side of the small and obviously newly allocated 'rest room'.
A week before, the staff room had housed the hotels Christmas and other seasonal decorations.

Mark continued while extending a hand "I'm Mark, this is nothing to worry about, it's Leonard isn't it? "

"Lenny" the man replied taking the indicated seat.

"Great. Tell me Lenny, when did you start work here"

Leonard looked at the ceiling briefly and then said, "It was summer back in 2010 that I started"
"That's great", Mark nodded and made a note, "And do you have a contract of employment?"

Leonard laughed "what's one of them? I don't know

anyone in town who does apart from a few of the managers of places."

Mark made another note and continued.

"What exactly do you do here Leonard, sorry, Lenny.

"I do a bit of everything really, cleaning and repairs and sometimes the bar. If it's busy I help in the kitchen and laundry and in the season, I do the mascot." Leonard paused.
"Everyone hates doing the mascot."

Mark asked Leonard to explain.

"Every time we do a cabaret or show or it's something like carnival week, the hotel has a mascot. Who-ever gets picked has to put on the outfit and give out leaflets and things." He seemed upset.

Mark made some more notes, Leonard clearly needed to get something off his chest.

"The outfit stinks, everyone hates it, and it's hot as hell in there and really sweaty and it never gets dry cleaned because they're too tight to send it to laundry" he gushed and then more slowly and with a lump in his throat "and it's normally me what gets picked"

Mark was reaching for his teacup but stopped abruptly as he realised the man in front of him was now holding back

tears.
He let Leonard finish.

"I absolutely hate it, and I get the piss taken everywhere in town, I'll never live it down"
With that, Leonard burst into tears.

Mark didn't know what to do. At times in the past the interviews had gotten emotional, even heated sometimes, as employees realised, they'd been getting abused and cheated.

It took over an hour and several cups of tea to get a full explanation.

All the big holiday parks and hotels had their own mascots. Polperro Play & Stay Park had their own Play and Stay Porpoise. Trepiddle had the Trepiddle Teddy. Cliff Caravan Park had the Cliff Caravan Crab.
There were dolphins and teddies and mackerel and even the famous Looe Lobster. They all had outfits and each place had some poor sod who had to put the things on and pose for photographs with snotty children while pretending to be enjoying the experience. These outfits were generally heavy, uncomfortable, itchy, hot to wear and virtually impossible to cleanse of the sweat and tears of the multiple previous occupants.

By the time the Looe view hotel had decided to follow suit, almost all the nautical options had been exhausted. Then some bright spark of a manager had been watching a pair of fishermen digging the riverbed at low tide for bait.

Lenny the Lugworm was born.

It was bad enough being the Caravan Club Crab, but no one on the planet wanted to be Lenny the bloody Lugworm. The fact in this case his real name was Leonard, made it all far worse.

Mark was relieved that this interview was over. It wasn't good for the staff having to recall their various traumas. It was also quite apparent that different members of staff were being paid markedly different rates. Some were being paid the minimum wage. Some, like Leonard, were being paid up to three pounds less an hour than they were entitled to and had been for some time.

Mark sighed inwardly. This culture of abuse occurred all over Cornwall. People were so desperate for work that they accepted it. In the meantime, the owners of the big businesses drove around in flash cars and lived in the most expensive houses. It was rotten to the core.
Mark was employed by the County Council. He uncovered wrongdoings every day. He wrote reports, made recommendations and petitioned his bosses to take legal action. Of course, it was an extremely rare occasion anyone was prosecuted, after all, the councillors and business owners were all cousins.

Mark had almost all the information he needed now regarding the Looe River View Hotel. He had already summoned the owners and managers to a meeting the following morning. This was the part of his job that he loved, the bit where he explained the law and what was required to set things straight. Quite often it meant employees received considerable pay rises and a hefty and hurried back payment. In twelve years in his job, he could count on one hand the number of occasions when he hadn't needed to make any recommendations at all. That nice lady in the Guildhall market for instance, she had been outstanding, or the chap who'd run the Beach Shack. Both had paid their staff above the normal rates and had really taken care of their people. Genuinely decent employers it seemed, were difficult to find.

He turned his thoughts to his next job. Several complaints had been made by departing employees and so he would now be starting discreet investigations into the workings of the Town Welcome and Tourist Support. This he mused would be an easy one for once, not many people in Looe thought very highly of the TWATS.

As afternoon passed into early evening, Donald's bladder caused him to wake with his usual set of moans and grumbles. He pulled himself off the comfortable hotel bed and mumbled to Sylvia who was now sitting up beside him reading a magazine.
"Hmm, bathroom, crickey my hips ache"
He shuffled off to the lavatory. A few minutes later the door was thrust open again and a startled looking Donald stood wide eyed and fully awake.
"Bloody hell Sylvia, it looks like a taxidermists parlour in here, what happened?"
Sylvia sat up fully and Donald noticed she was wearing her special silk dressing gown.
"I made myself all smooth for you Donald" she smiled seductively. "I didn't want to wake you, I'll tidy up in a while, come to bed darling"
"Smooth! Hells bells, it looks like someone shaved a badger in there" Donald sputtered.
Sylvia smiled again and indicated the lower half of her gown and winked.
"I've shaved my badger especially for you Donald" she pulled back the bedclothes "Now then, are you coming?"

A few doors down the corridor, Marjorie was emerging from her bathroom.
Norman looked up sympathetically.
"Is that better now love?"

"Oh much" she answered looking sincere. "Just like a Cumberland it was. All is well in the world again, I feel much lighter"
"Oh good, I'm glad. I think I might go and build a small island myself in a minute"
Marjorie nodded in approval.

"Thanks for not rushing me this time."

Neither could remember at just what stage in their marriage they'd begun discussing their bowels. It was one of their everyday conversations now. If ever one of them had been admitted to hospital, that was one bodily function the other was completely up to date with. Some couples got on better if they slept in separate beds. For Norman and Marjorie, the real breakthrough had come when they'd had a second toilet fitted in their comfortable bungalow.

Over the years, the magic of synchronicity had worked on them. Tensions had risen while one or the other hopped from foot to foot waiting for the sitter to vacate the throne. Toilet number two had restored harmony to their home. As soon as Norman thought it, Marjorie vocalised,
"Do you think there's more than one lavatory in that apartment?"
Norman quickly answered.
"If there isn't, it'll be worth every penny to get another put in"
Marjorie smiled at him appreciatively. These things were important.

Norman held up the Town Welcome and Tourist Support magazine.

"If that place is the right one for us, there's certainly plenty going on. It looks like they've got a busy social calendar here, have a listen?"
He began to list the events.
"This is just Easter. Giant easter Egg hunt for kids plus hidden beer and prosecco bottles for mums and dads, Easter Sunday on the beach. Separate enclosures. That

sounds like fun"
Marjorie laughed "What a splendid idea, shall we go?"
Norman continued.
"Easter parade. Looe River View Hotel Easter cabaret. Looe environmental group beach clean and talk. Town Welcome and Tourist Support open day, come and explore the Old-fish-waste-cellar. Looe Easter fancy dress fun run"
Norman paused before adding indignantly.
"The words fun and run do not belong in the same sentence together. There's only ever two good reasons for running"
Marjorie had heard him make this speech before and finished for him.
"Yes love, if someone is chasing you with an axe and last orders"
Norman laughed while nodding his approval. He looked back at the magazine and continued.
"Looe hotel and holiday camps mascot race. Hmm, I wonder what that is? Oh, it's in the summer."
Marjorie ran her hand over the sheet "Come to bed darling"
Norman did as he'd been asked.

As dawn broke on Good Friday, Morley Sprygelly put the bag containing his outfit on the back seat of his car before settling himself in the driver's seat for the short trip back to his beloved hometown.
He missed Looe more than he would allow himself to admit. His pasties had been a great success in Bristol, and the realities of business meant he had a far better chance of building a pension there than back at home where a small handful of people dominated the landscape.
Some of them were his relatives.
Besides that, the fluctuating seasonal footfall meant in holiday times there were weeks of abundance, but this was always interspersed by months of scarcity as far as regular income was concerned. One day, when he'd earned enough, he would happily move back.

He visited as often as he could and when he did, kept seeing vacant shops and other businesses with leases for sale all over the town. He frowned as he thought about all the hopeful couples who had come to the town with a dream of running a tearoom or a souvenir shop. Few managed to last more than two seasons. Most left again, broke and disillusioned. Those who stayed ended up working for the people who had been their business competitors. They worked for poor wages and quite often ended up living in poorly maintained accommodation. This was an aspect the tourists never got to see.
Some people in the town were doing very well, a great many more were hanging on by their fingernails.
Some were truly lovely people, honest and sincere, and then there were the others. There were the cliques and clubs and fraternities, the back stabbers, the gossip mongers, and the downright dishonest.
Morley had decided to bypass all of that, but he'd wept

when he left. He thought of Looe as being like a beautiful cheese, there was so much to savour and enjoy, but there was also a layer which was completely unpalatable.

He turned his thoughts back to the journey and tuned into greatest Hit's radio. He'd have to cross the Tamar bridge before he could tune into Radio Cornwall. He'd tried other local radio stations in the past. Radio Devon was like something from a bad 1950's B-movie and Radio Somerset could induce highway hypnosis within minutes. As he drove, he'd do his best to get into character he thought, he wanted to be a good Jesus.
The radio played the Stranglers 'Hanging around'


In their hotel room, Sylvia turned on the bedside lamp and leaned over to kiss Donald on the forehead.
"Oh, please love, no more, I can't take it" he blurted out.
"Oh Donald, you silly sod, that was quite enough for me last night thank you" and then added sweetly as she stroked his face "My stallion".
Sylvia got up and deftly flicked the little button- on the kettle.
"I thought I might go down to the early morning workout group. They have one in the gym every morning before breakfast especially for older people it says on the door".
Donald looked relieved.
"Oh I see, is that what you and Marjorie decided in the bar last night?"
Norman decided not to mention that he'd heard the barman talking to the receptionist as the pair had laughed at the previous days Jerkasize class.
"Poor old buggers, not a good hip between them, there's more metal in that lot than in the Blackpool tower." She'd

said. "We ought to call it shuffle-a-sizes."

The ladies had sipped cocktails in the window of the hotel bar while Donald and Norman had gotten better acquainted. They were almost the same age with Norman being just a week younger.
In addition to being special club members, they also shared mutual interests in wood turning, Glastonbury festival, 70's music, archaeology, bowling, and cultivating marijuana. They'd both been almost forty when trance music had become popular, but it transpired that age was no barrier in the Rave scene, and they'd even been at some of the same ones at the same time.

Sylvia and Marjorie were getting along splendidly too. Like their husbands, they were determined to be evergreens. They both loved to dance, and Marjorie had confided that she and her husband subscribed to Red Eye magazine even now. Sylvia was heartily impressed to learn that Marjorie at 74 years old, still earned a good commission hosting sex toys sales parties.

Both couples had enjoyed their evening although it was much later than they were all used to these days. Donald and Sylvia hadn't climbed into bed until almost 9.30.
Sylvia began to squeeze herself into her fluorescent lycra. Donald could feel himself beginning to get warmer as he looked on. Pulling back the bed clothes he gently pulled himself upright, gave his wife a quick Woo-Woo, and made his way into the bathroom.
"What time is it?" he asked through the open door.
"It's quarter to seven" Sylvia answered cheerfully.
"Oh my god woman, are you completely stark raving bonkers? It's the middle of the bloody night"

"Oh Donald, don't be grumpy, we've got an exciting day ahead" came the reply as Sylvia bent to tie up the laces on her plimsoles. "We can go back to bed later, how about a little afternoon delight?"

Donald made a mental note to try and find himself some oysters if he could. The blue pills from the chemist had helped a bit, but his libido was no match for Sylvias, and he'd need all the help he could get.
Donald and Sylvia were as in love as they had been since the day they'd married. Donald still fancied Sylvia, he just didn't have the same urges anymore. He did his best to hide it from Sylvia and show himself to be as committed to their sex life as he'd ever been. He hated the thought that she might tire of him and go looking for a younger man. It was exhausting though, especially as these days, 'getting lucky' meant having an afternoon nap without the bloody phone ringing.

At the town's single platform railway station, Alan and Eileen waited for the train. Alan had told Eileen that he planned to go to the cabaret with Ryan but omitted the part that they'd be joining in the fancy dress. Eileen was pleased that Alan was going to start venturing out socially again. More than once she'd said to him.
"For goodness' sake Alan, go to the pub, have a drink, you haven't seen your friends for weeks"

Clearly the incident at the Special club, whatever it was, had left him deeply traumatised. He had barely left Emmety Villa in the following months, preferring to immerse himself in the large garden with projects he'd invented.

Eileen was going to a school reunion in Wiltshire for the weekend. She'd been born in Looe, but her family had been involved in running bars all over the country, including one in Chippenham while she went to secondary school. Eileen had left home at 17 and had made her way back to Looe. Nowhere compared to home.

Alan could have gone with her but they'd both decided that he'd probably be bored silly while Eileen reminisced with her friends and bopped the night away to late eighties music.
Besides that, someone had to stay and look after their two cats.
Just like Donald and Sylvia, they were deeply in love, and just like Norman and Marjorie, they understood that sometimes it was good for both of them to spend a little time apart.

Alan checked his watch.
"We're far too early, it isn't due for half an hour yet"
Eileen gave him a conciliatory smile.
"Sorry love, I forgot the times change at Easter"
As she was speaking, at the back of the police station next door, Cousin Veryan was opening the back door to let Cousin Lowenna in. Lowenna spotted her cousins hovering at the end of the platform.
"Oh, hello you two, off somewhere nice?" Veryan peeked around the door to see who Lowenna was talking to and added,
"Oh, hiya, have you got to wait long? Schedule changes today. I've got coffee on if you fancy?"
Alan was delighted and picked up Eileen's suitcase.
"Brilliant, we'll be right round."

It wasn't long before all four were sitting in Lowanna's office with four steaming mugs.
Eileen had already told the girls about her trip away and explained that Alan was staying.
"You will keep an eye on him, won't you?" She asked her uniformed cousins.
Alan laughed nervously.
"I don't imagine for a minute anything the least bit 'unusual' will happen this weekend." he said with a slight waiver in his voice. "Anyway, what's on? You're both in early?"

"Busy day for us" Veryan answered.
Lowenna, added a few details.
"Easter parade, first busy weekend of the season and all

that. You know how it is, never a dull moment"

The truth was that even with the towns incredibly fast rumour machine, most people only ever got to know a fraction of what was going on, especially where the police were concerned. Sargent Lowenna was in early to make sure the 'Oaf wagon' as it was referred to, was delivered by lunchtime. There were certain to be a few candidates for a ride in it later.
The conversation ebbed and flowed as various celebrities in the town were discussed.

The conversation was interrupted by a loud buzzing from the back door. Veryan went to investigate and came back with Cousin Morley. There was a round of hugs. Lowenna stifled a laugh. You couldn't get much more Looe-like than this, five cousins in one room, two of them colleagues and two of them married.

Elsewhere across the town, things which had hibernated all winter were now coming to life. Cafes, souvenir shops, the TWATS office and the museum all had a flurry of activity as the owners and staff took a deep breath before the plunge into the new season. Window frames and tables had fresh paint, china had been replenished, fridge magnets had been topped up and the town was ready-ish.

On the rooftops and lampposts, herring gulls made ready. Their heightened instincts told them a fresh shoal was on its way. This wasn't an aquatic shoal; it would be a shoal of chips and ice creams and pasties. When it came to predators, there were few things on the planet that could match a herring gull intent on catching a pasty.

Cowboy began to stir in his bed. At first, he thought he'd pulled the night before although he couldn't remember what had happened. This wouldn't be the first such occasion. He'd have to get rid of her. Crickey! He took in the long silver hair on the pillow beside him. How old was she? And why was she wearing one of his girlfriend's nighties?
He needed to get her out of there and sharpish at that.
He was about to shake her shoulder when she rolled over and farted.

It was Uncle Keith.
"Oh my god" Cowboy groaned to himself, just as quickly he realised, he was still fully clothed. He even had his white slip on's on still.

Uncle Keith had his eyes open now. Cowboy stumbled out of the bed hurriedly.
"What the 'ells goin on?"

A bleary eyed Keith stared back at him.
"I dunno mate, I can't remember anything after that second litre of voddy"
"What the 'ell is you wearing? And why the 'ell were you in my bed?"
"From what I remember" Uncle Keith sighed "You told me to use this one, you wuz going to sleep on the sofa downstairs"
Cowboy had a vague recollection of waking up in the night and finding himself on a sofa in the kitchen. Freezing cold and still plastered, he'd clambered up the stairs and climbed into bed with his girlfriend, except that it was Keith, not his missis.
He fixed Keith with a firm stare.
"We are never, ever, going to mention this again"


Jimmy was awake too. He'd be glad to get out of his tiny, rented flat in the town centre. It had been good for a while and it was close to work, but Jimmy had grown tired of listening to the late-night drunks and their shouting. He had to be in work at 6.30 most mornings to go and take over from the night fill crew. He'd grown tired of the regular 3am

"Julie, Julie, come back. I'm sorry, I didn't mean it." or the rattle of dustbins being thrown around to snarls of
"I'm gonna kick your bleedin teef in."
He'd rung the police control room so many times that now when he rang, he was answered with a courteous
"Hello James, what's happening in Looe tonight then?"

His appointment to view the apartments was at 10am. He had already decided he liked the one on the top floor. No

one overhead to stomp around he thought.
The estate agent had rung to say that there were other perspective purchasers at 10.30, so please be punctual. Jimmy was rather affronted; Jimmy was never late for anything. His phone beeped; it was Rachael. Jimmy realised that Joyce must have passed on his number.
"Can't wait to see you later. xxx"
Jimmy put his phone back on the bedside cabinet, he realised he was trembling.

Breakfast in the Looe River View hotel followed the same pattern as the previous morning. The usually socially conscious and law-abiding senior citizens did everything they could to consume and pocket as much as they could in the dining room.

The long-life muffins were always a favourite. When Uncle Denzel had a say, the muffins would be available only on request. Paul Sprygelly on the other hand, knew that if the old codgers filled up on muffins, there was a far lower likelihood of reception receiving multiple requests for laxatives and haemorrhoid creams. Paul dreaded to think what chemicals were in them. He certainly never ate them himself.
The hotel wasn't allowed to supply medications and it negated hours of repeatedly having to explain this and to deny requests for members of staff to 'just nip out to the chemist'.

On the first two mornings of a group visit such as this, the Muffins basket would be filled at least four times. By day-three, the elderly visitors were generally fed up with them. The whole business was a pantomime and the hotel staff managed to gracefully work around it.

One or two of the more determined old gits, as they were never referred to in the hotel, would always try and get into the dining room in the small hours of the morning. Others would arrive half an hour before serving began. By the time breakfast was in full flow, in between running around to meet the numerous demands of their visitors, the staff would be frequently and discreetly scooping up muffins which had slipped out of pockets or sleeves or not fitted into already crammed handbags.

Because they were individually wrapped, they would simply be returned to a box in the hotel's considerable larder. When the valued guests departed, housekeeping would collect another three or four boxes of muffins that had been abandoned in the hotel rooms.
Paul liked to call it the 'Muffin-go-round'

Freshly showered and powdered, Sylvia and Marjorie had joined their husbands for breakfast and now with stomachs, bladders and pockets filled to bursting, they made their final preparations for the viewing of Emmety Villa.

"It's an unusual name don't you think?" Marjorie commented.
"I expect it's something in Cornish" Sylvia offered.
Norman beckoned Paul to the table and asked,
"We're going to a place called Emmety Villa, don't suppose you know it do you? What does Emmety mean, is it Cornish?"
Paul was a little startled. Emmety Villa was the building where Uncle Denzel and that weird bloke had been arrested. The name had always been a source of amusement in the town.
"I don't know the place myself" he answered diplomatically "But I think Emmet means 'welcome visitor' in old Cornish."
Norman seemed satisfied, so Paul excused himself. He walked hurriedly to the kitchen doors and just made it inside as he began to laugh hysterically.

The couples agreed to meet in the reception area and walk to Emmety Villa together, first they needed to empty their latest pilfering's. Marjorie's handbag was full of sachets of brown sugar, both men had plastic bags containing bacon and sausages in their pockets, and Sylvia had been collecting bread rolls.

.

Rachael was already waiting at the bottom of the steps which led up to Emmety Villa, when Jimmy and the young estate agent arrived. Jimmy had gone to school with Peter, and they still saw one another regularly as Peter shopped in the small supermarket. Peter had seen Jimmy walking and stopped just down the road. As he carefully brought his car to a stop, Rachael waved rather excitedly to Jimmy.

"Isn't she lovely?" Jimmy said with a sigh "She's a work of art" he continued.
Peter took in Rachael's rotund little body and shockingly short skirt and silently agreed. She was indeed a work of art, if only he could remember the name of that Picasso painting.

Jimmy was only halfway out of the passenger seat when Rachael stepped forward and wrapped her pudgy fingers around his own moist hand. She leaned towards him to kiss him. Taken off-guard by her unexpected forwardness, he jerked his head back, banging it on the top corner of the car door. Rachael missed her target, which had been Jimmy's mouth, and managed to kiss him squarely on his upturned nostrils.
Peter came to Jimmy's rescue and extended his hand to Rachael.
"Hello, I'm Peter, it's Rachael isn't it? I'll be showing you around today."
Rachael was delighted to have been recognised until just as he was extending his hand Peter added,
"Do you still work at Pigs R Us?"
Rachael grasped the proffered hand and squeezed with a

vice like grip as she answered between clenched teeth.
"I haven't worked there for over ten years. I'm in television now."
Peter desperately tried to take his hand away, but Rachael had a grip tighter than a Cornishman with a pound coin at a car-boot sale.
"Oh, how wonderful" he sputtered "Sorry, I never watch telly, I only ever look at you tube"

Rachael finally let go. Peter did his best to remain calm while his circulation restored itself.
"Why is there scaffolding around the building?" Rachael asked.
Peter explained that for several years, the owner of the freehold had neglected his responsibilities in maintaining the property. Following certain legal actions in the town, being careful not to mention Denzel Sprygelly by name, there had been a sudden flurry of activity as errant landlords had realised, they were no longer immune to prosecution.

Emmety Villa had a new roof and was about to be painted. The garden walls were about to be rebuilt where they had begun to collapse, and the drains had all been dug out and re-lined. It had been expensive for the freeholder, and a huge relief to the lease holders who could now sleep peacefully.
"I think it's that chap Cowboy who's doing the work, those are his stores." Peter pointed to the block of stone-built garages attached to the property.

"Shall we go up?" he gestured towards the steps. As all three of them looked up at Emmety Villa, they clearly saw Alan rapidly stepping back from the blinded window inside his middle floor apartment.
A few moments later, Alan intercepted the trio of visitors as they reached the front door. He immediately recognised Jimmy of course and Rachael was delighted when he said "Eileen and me watch you on the telly almost every night"

Rachael gave Alan her best smile. Peter thought she looked rather like a Boa constrictor eyeing up a goat, a noticeably short Boa constrictor at that.

Alan remembered Peter from the initial taking of details by the estate agents. Alan held all the keys and so it was Alan who had let Peter into the building on those occasions too. As they thanked him for letting them in, all three visitors did their best to avert their eyes from the colourful silk slippers Alan was wearing. The toes curled up into points and they had little silver stars sown onto them.

As he made his way back into his flat, Alan could hear his phone ringing. He realised with horror that he'd been so preoccupied with tonight's cabaret that he'd completely forgotten he was due to help with the Easter parade.
He managed to answer just as the answerphone clicked in.

"Yes, yes of course, sorry, I'll be right there, I'm leaving right now".

He grabbed his jacket and car keys and set off for the

church hall. He was just about to get into the car when he realised, he still had his wizard's slippers on. He groaned and then dashed back up the steps, almost colliding with Peter in the hallway as he showed Jimmy and Rachael into the other downstairs apartment.

"Sorry, so sorry, forgot my erm…."

Alan decided not to finish and made off for the stairs to his front door.
The three visitors sniggered as they entered flat 2.

"I wonder what all that was about?" Peter vocalised and then quickly added. "He's a nice chap, I expect he's a really good neighbour"

By the time Alan arrived at the Church hall, an anxious crowd had gathered. He was supposed to have opened at 9am. The parade was due to begin at 11am and it was almost 10.15 now.

The vicar was clearly irritated, and Cousin Morley was dressed only in a loin cloth made from old bandages and a crown of genuine thorns. The poor man was freezing.

It was Alans's job to open the hall so that the rest of Jesus's escort could get dressed in their costumes and then to transport the large balsa wood crucifix and Jesus to the beginning of the parade route.

"Hurry up, hurry up man" urged the vicar.

Alan fumbled with keys as he frantically tried to unlock the door. At last, it sprung open and around twenty people rushed past Alan and into the main hall.

The vicar was clearly not impressed and reached inside his cassock to retrieve his impressive 1-pint hip flask. He took a long pull on it before offering it to Alan by way of apology.

"It's rum. Alan, you must never do that to me again, I was praying as if I was trying to save a politician. My poor nerves just don't cope well with deviations from plans"

Alan handed back the flask. The vicar continued

"Anyway, let's get on with our day, shall we? Would you mind giving me a lift? "

A flurry of activity echoed in the hall as volunteers dragged boxes from under the stage and attempted to swiftly dress themselves as centurions and disciples.

Mary Magdalene and Mary, mother of Jesus began arguing over who was going to wear the blue robe. It was an old argument and the two women had been contesting the role for several years. It usually took the intervention of Jesus to sort out the dispute.
Someone had loaned Morley an overcoat now. He joined the Vicar and the secret wizard and accepted the hip flask.

"I'm frozen" he shivered "I hope it's not windy down there. Hopefully, I can warm up a bit once we start walking"

Alan and the vicar nodded in sympathy. The giant crucifix was balsa wood, but even that became a load for whoever had volunteered to drag it from the little church, all the way along West Looe Quay, over the bridge, and back down the other side of the river to the seafront.

All those involved took the Easter parade very seriously. They all did their best to embrace their roles and put on the best show they could. Jesus's crown of thorns was just one example, the blood currently running slowly down his face, was real.

Sometimes one or two of the centurions got carried away too. It had been decided several years ago to dispense with the famed spear of Longinus after an unfortunate incident on the route. It was important to keep an eye on them, they had new whips this year. The vicar had found them in one of the charity shops. Alan winced as he realised, he'd seen them before, they had belonged to Maurice.

With the crucifix strapped to the roof of the car, the vicar and Jesus in the back, and the winner of the Mary-Mother-of-Jesus' contest perched in the passenger seat, Alan put his foot down and scared about a dozen other motorists on his slightly inebriated rush to get to the quay.
The vicar was feeling the effects of the rum now and wanted to sing car songs. Both Jesus and Mary knew the words and joined in cheerfully.
As they drove down St Matins hill, the words of 'Beer is best' reverberated around the vehicle.

Jimmy and Rachael were leaving just as Norman and Marjorie and Donald and Sylvia arrived at Emmety Villa for their viewing.

Jimmy had told the agent he'd take the top flat on the spot. It was exactly what he was looking for and long hours and frugal living, plus a recent inheritance, meant he could pay cash if his offer to pay the full asking price was accepted. Rachael had been most impressed to learn that not only was Jimmy solvent, but he was also clearly able to manage his finances, unlike some of the other competitors for her affections in the town.

"My place is only five minutes away" she fluttered her eyelashes at him. She gripped his hand firmly as she steered him into turning right at the bottom of the steps. "Let's go and have some lunch to celebrate" Jimmy nodded compliantly. Never mind butterflies, he felt he had a herd of donkeys performing acrobatics in his stomach.

Rachael knew that she didn't have anything suitable for lunch back at her little flat, except a few bottles of Moet that she'd accumulated. It didn't matter she thought, the only thing she planned on devouring was Jimmy. Jimmy didn't have to go back to work until Sunday and she wasn't due to be back to the television station building until Tuesday.

It was, she thought, going to be a very memorable and wonderful Good Friday indeed.

Jimmy simply followed her lead. He was completely enamoured with her, and terrified.

Meanwhile, Peter was busy welcoming the two older

couples and indicating that they should follow him inside. Norman wanted to know if they would be allowed to erect a poly-tunnel at the top of the communal garden. He and Donald had already discussed whether it was a suitable place to grow their assorted strains of Sativas and Indicas. Peter thought this might be possible if the other residents didn't object. Norman was clearly pleased.

The viewing went well. Both couples favoured different apartments which fortunately turned out to be the ones they'd already decided upon.

The one Marjorie liked even had a second toilet already in place. She was silently relieved. She produced some truly monstrous extrusions these days, and that was one aspect of life that she certainly didn't want to share with her husband. If Donald knew, then it would be highly likely that everyone down at the local pub would know too. Her only concern was that both apartments and the corridor between them, seemed to hold a lingering aroma of rubber and baby oil.

Sylvia had loved the views of the valley. From the kitchen in her preferred apartment, with a good pair of binoculars, she'd be able to see right inside most of the neighbouring windows. Sylvia did like to know what was going on around her. Back at home her nickname was 'The neighbourhood watch'. Sylvia had noticed the aroma too. It reminded her of the storeroom back at home in the charity shop.

Donald and Norman had been nonchalant about which apartment was preferrable, accepting that either was fine by them. Their interest was on the garden, the nearby facilities, and the opportunity to put up sheds and growing areas. There was an area of woodland bordering the garden which Peter had said, 'no one knew who it belonged to'.
He'd also said that he'd walked up there to take photographs of the outside of Emmety Villa and the river. It didn't look as if anyone at all ever ventured into the wood these days and all the neighbouring gardens had high fences or hedges.
Both men had visions of a secluded clearing filled with growbags where they could nurture their 'ornamental Jamaican stinging nettles'. It was a name they both used when inquisitive relatives asked too many questions.

Leaving an incredibly happy Peter to lock up, the two couples set off back down the steps.
Marjorie was the first to speak.

"I think I could be really happy here"

Donald agreed. They had enough money saved to move, and his contacts at his branch of the Special Club would make sure all the conveyancing went through smoothly. Selling their old house wouldn't present any issues. Properties around them were snapped up within days normally. His only concerns were his sizable forest of marijuana plants growing in the grounds of the old primary school which backed on to his garden.
The site was marked for development but again, his

connections at the Special Club meant that the land had never been placed on the market up to now. Regrettably, it would have to be an early harvest.

Norman quite liked the look of the closest pub. 'Thunderstruck' had been blasting out of the open door when he'd walked past earlier, and a young man of around 50 clad in bikers' leathers, had been standing in the doorway smoking a joint. At 74 years old, that was his kind of watering hole. He would talk to Sylvia in private and then, in all likelihood, make an offer before the Estate agent closed for the day.

Lowenna clicked on her radio.

"I'm on the bridge, all clear love, let them go"

Veryan could just make out the flashing lights of her sergeant's police car which was preventing traffic from driving down the quay until the parade had passed. It never ceased to amaze either Veryan or Lowenna just how many people thought it was okay to try to drive through the Easter parade, the carnival procession, or any of the other many events that safety dictated the road be closed for ten minutes.

It was difficult enough stewarding the Emmets, most of these clowns were local. Lowenna tutted to herself, they really ought to know better. There was always some prat who thought they were more important than everybody else.

Veryan raised a hand to signal all clear to the parade, and Jesus began his long painful journey to the hill of Golgotha. In reality this meant a long walk to the beach, but it was almost the same thing.

The single drummer began his slow, sorrowful whacking of his instrument as four centurions hastily finished their cans of cider and crammed them into a bin on the quay. They had to run to catch up with Jesus who was making good progress and rapidly getting away from them.

Behind Jesus and the drummer, and slightly out of the pre-arranged placements, the two Mary's followed, both busily trying to out-wail one another.

The centurions caught up and almost sent Mary Magdalene flying into the river when one of them collided with her. They waved their whips in the air excitedly.

One of the men brandished his whip a little too enthusiastically and caught Jesus across his shoulders. A bright red welt began to appear almost instantly. Jesus paused in the middle of the road and fixed the centurion with a look that could have frozen helium.

"If you do that again chum, I'm going to punch your flaming lights out. Got it?"

Without waiting for the man to answer, he picked up the crucifix again and continued towards the bridge. After that, all four centurions continued to wave the bondage whips, but rather flaccidly, and they all stayed a respectful distance behind the saviour of mankind.

As the parade drew closer to the Looe River View Hotel, Mark Wray was finishing his conversation with Paul.

"So just to clarify, you manage the dining room, the ordering, the bar, housekeeping, bookings and reception, stores and orders, laundry, staff scheduling and payroll. Is that everything?"

Paul thought about his daily routine.

"Sometimes I organise the entertainment and of course we all step in and out of the kitchen when required"

Mark frowned. He'd been looking into the number of hours Paul continually worked and decided that clearly, Paul was being exploited like a Victorian, as were most of the rest of the employees.

Times had moved on, and so had legislation. Mark would be drafting his address to the hotels owners this lunchtime. They'd been summoned to present themselves in the morning.

After breakfast, the hotel would temporarily switch to skeletal staffing while everyone else met in the dining room. Mark and Paul and the rest of the employees were going to enjoy the meeting far more than the owners and managers.

Mark said his goodbye and still gazing at his notebook, stepped out straight into the path of the Messiah.

Jesus almost stumbled into the suited figure. He managed to right his burden just before it toppled to the tarmac.

"Oi watch it chum! You've got eyes in your head, try looking where you're going every now and then will you? Pillock!"

At that point Jesus and Mark made eye contact. Mark had done his work experience with Morley. Both men smiled broadly at one another. Mark replied to the challenge.
"Oh? Pillock is it? And I thought we were friends"
Jesus turned to Mary Magdalene and pushed the huge crucifix at her.

"Hold this a minute, will you?"

He turned back to Mark and the two embraced.

"Oh Mark, so good to see you fella. I sincerely hope you're keeping up the good work?"

"I am Morley, you look well mate, apart from the blood and the…, that's not make up….is that a whip mark?"

The parade had come to an abrupt halt, which due to the protrusion of the hotel and a curve in the road, meant most of the followers couldn't see the cause of the obstruction. Sensing an opportunity, the four centurions wasted no time in dashing into the bar and ordering 4 pints of lager.

"Get me one in a plastic, will you?" The drummer called after them.

For the next few minutes, Mark and Jesus continued to exchange pleasantries until the vicar stomped up and interrupted the meeting. He could see Lowenna beckoning the parade forward as two queues of impatient traffic got even longer as they waited for the quay to clear.

"I'll catch you later if you're around, must dash"
Jesus bade Mark goodbye and took the crucifix back from a relieved looking Mary.
The four centurions finished quaffing their pints and tumbled back into the street to re-join the parade. The smartly dressed, bewildered crowd representing the local parishioners, resumed the slow shuffle along the waterside. The drummer, newly revived with a pint of The Looe River

Views strongest, began to beat with a rhythm far more appropriate to a New Orleans jazz club.

Right at the back, doing her best not to giggle into her radio, Veryan was explaining to Lowenna what had just happened.

"Let's just get them over the bridge" Lowenna answered cheerfully. "Once they're on Fore Street they can manage without us."

Lowenna looked toward the head end of the parade. Jesus was looking suitably harried, as did Mary Magdalene and the cluster of disciples. The drummer and the four centurions however, appeared to be boogying their way along the quay. Lowenna smiled to herself. Despite the queues of irritated motorists now shooting her annoyed death stares, things were going quite well this year.

As the head of the parade approached the bridge, the rest of the town began to buzz with bank holiday activity. Delighted gulls looked on as the first shoal of pasties of the season worked its way from little cave-like hatcheries, out onto the pavements and down towards the seafront. The ambient noise level in the town had increased by around 40 decibels. Puzzled motorists navigated the one-way system anxiously having completely missed the six-foot wide 'Access only' signs. Shopkeepers bagged up fridge magnets, relieved that at last the six-month financial drought of the long winter was coming to an end.

In the Petrie Dish Café, Ronald thumped the side of the dishwasher again. It had been a busy morning for the first time in months and he needed to clear the overheated machine as fast as possible. Sticky plates and piles of used coffee cups threatened to topple over at the end of the counter. The dishwasher was both leaking and failing to get the contents thoroughly cleaned. The floor was gradually becoming more slippery, and the orders were coming in so fast that there was no time to mop up. Ronald consoled himself that at least he wouldn't have to face a hygiene inspection. The local council had trimmed that department into almost extinction, and so unlike previous years, the café could genuinely live up to its name.

The naming of the café had caused a ripple of amusement all over the town and to a few of the sharper visitors. Ronald had never been good with common sayings. He often used to say things like 'Once a leopard, always a leopard' or 'It's no use getting upset over things that get spilt in the dairy'. A particular favourite was "I have to visit a friend who knows about canines".
That one left quite a few people scratching their heads. Most people assumed that it was a common expression in Milton Keynes and so allowed Ronald to express himself while sniggering at him behind his back.

When Ronald had first come to the town, he'd driven past a pub in Liskeard called 'The Great Pot' and thought what a great name that was. He'd picked The Petrie Dish himself and never really understood what the true purpose of that item of scientific equipment was. It was an appropriate name for the café. For instance, nowhere else in town could you see the spectacle of grey dishcloths being laid out to dry on top of the Barista machine. The mop bucket contained more deadly bacteria than Porton Down.

Ronald thumped the side of the dishwasher again; he'd have to get someone in to fix it. He looked up at his new crew, hopefully they would be fully trained by the summer and then he could go and pursue his other dreams. Like almost everyone else currently serving up food and drink to the visitors, Ronald had big plans.

Back at the bridge, Jesus had at last come to East Looe and was turning into Fore Street with a slow and weary trudge. He lifted his gaze from the tarmac and was immediately drawn to the window of the nearby bakery. At this point, professional interest overcame him, and he marched straight over to the window of the shop for a better look. He and the current owner had been business partners several years before, and they remained friends now. Jesus gazed at the pasties and chelsea buns, they were magnificent. Undoubtedly the best in town, and unlike the offerings from the Petrie Dish, consumable without unpleasant consequences.

Puzzled pedestrians who hadn't seen the rest of the parade yet, looked on as Jesus involuntarily licked his lips. His appreciation was interrupted when he heard the voice of the vicar shouting

"Clear the way for the soldiers of the Roman empire!"

Jesus quickly came back to the present moment, hoisted up the crucifix, and began to trudge once more. He could come back and grab a pasty after they had finished nailing him up.

Curious to see what was going to happen, visitors began to join the crowd of parishioners as they too passed the bakery with anticipatory glances in through the window. The vicar decided to pause until everyone had passed, hoping that no one would notice if he had another swig from his hipflask.

Content that their part was done, Veryan and Lowenna began to get the traffic moving again. It would take about half an hour until the flow was restored entirely.

A lot of the motorists were unaware of what had caused the delay, a few understood what was going on and some of them were a little pressed for time.

Karen fell into the last category. She'd been scheduled to have a day off and been heading out to her favourite beach at Portwrinkle. Her phone had beeped with a text just as she was driving out of town, and so she'd stopped in a layby just in case it was her daughter.

It wasn't, it was her boss 'No chef today, can you come in?'. Loyal to a fault, Karen had messaged back to say she'd be there in half an hour and turned her car around to go home and collect her freshly laundered whites.

By the time she turned onto Fore Street, Jesus was about 200 yards ahead and out of sight. All that Karen could see was a big crowd of people all facing away from her, moving at a snail's pace towards the main town centre. She needed to get through the one-way system and down to her flat on the quay.  The people in front of her continued to dawdle in the road. She began tooting her horn. A man right at the back of the crowd hurriedly stuffed a hipflask back inside his cassock and came back to speak to her. As she lowered her window he leaned down and in a blast of rum informed her.

"Don't worry my child, we'll all get to our intended destinations as god intended"

"You'll get there well ahead of everyone if you don't get out of the flaming way" Karen snapped back at him and began to ease her car forward.

The crowd of parishioners and visitors parted slightly as Karen made her way forward. She could hear drumming now. She liked a bit of Samba. It was only when she'd gone another 100 yards that she began to see disciples and centurions. She looked ahead in horror as Jesus became visible by the bend in the road at the Guildhall. She pulled over to the kerb and as the vicar caught up with her again, leaned out of the window.

"I'm so sorry, I really am"

The vicar snapped back petulantly.

"Well, I might forgive you, or I might not" and marched off.
Karen was still by the curb laughing ten minutes later.

As the road ahead narrowed and the volume of pedestrians opposing the parade increased, Jesus long march became even slower. This suited the centurions, and the drummer was now nipping into every pub they passed for a quick one too. At the Galleon, the vicar was just on his way in, as the quintet was on their way out. Both Marys were at the bar and so were at least half a dozen disciples. It was like New Year's Eve.

Knowing the parade was almost at the seafront, and that Fridays was pensioner discount day in the Old Trawler, several of the parishioners also made a quick stop for refreshment.

By the time everyone had re-joined the rather beleaguered Jesus, rather than the sombre parade which had been intended, the whole street had something of a carnival atmosphere.

At last, the actors completed their long walk to the beach. The vicar began to read to the crowd about the great sacrifice Jesus was about to make.
Laying the crucifix on the sand, the centurions lashed Jesus to it with special ropes which weren't supposed to dig into his flesh. As the assembled crowd began to sing 'Alas! and Did My Saviour Bleed" They hoisted the crucifix until it was upright, and the base sunk firmly into the sand looking out to sea.
Behind Jesus, the singing ended, and the vicar implored everyone to join him in church on Sunday. The crowd applauded and began to disperse, most of them eager now

to get back to the pub. Even the two Marys left. Full bladders over-rode religious devotions no matter what they were.

Around ten minutes after everyone had gone, a rather chilly Morley called softly "Lads, are you going to let me down now? Lads?"
No one answered.

Cowboy and Uncle Keith were rummaging through the menswear rack in one of the charity shops. Cowboy knew it wouldn't be long until Keith wandered over to the other side of the shop and began to look at the dresses. Everyone knew that Keith just wanted to look pretty, and in these modern times, no one batted an eye anymore. When Keith appeared dressed as Tina Turner or Cher or Nicola Sturgeon, it didn't even get a mention. Keith liked wearing frocks, and that was that.

He had plenty of company in this. It seemed to Cowboy that more than half the blokes who drank in the Trawlerman's took every opportunity they could to put on a dress. At one point the town had had Pirate days. Those who wanted to would dress up and shuffle mock peg-legs from pub-to-pub Aarr-ing and talking to their model parrots. Things had changed over the last three years though, and so many of the blokes had opted to go as wenches, that eventually the pirate theme had been dropped altogether. Now every Sunday from April to October, it was getting increasingly rare to see men dressed as men in at least two of the pubs.

Just last Sunday Cowboy had been involved in a surreal conversation with a John the roofer, Peter the scaffolder and George the painter.
John had been dressed as Dorothy from the Wizard of Oz, Peter was Princess Leia and George was clad in satin and sequins dressed as a mermaid. They'd been discussing how to get timber, blocks and cement up 52 steps to the job they were all working on at Emmety Villa. The mermaid

and Dorothy had both been smoking cigars while swigging from pints of Guinness.

All of this was treated as completely normal, and the glittering trio hadn't even given explanations as to why they were dressed like that, it just happened to be Sunday. Things had changed a lot in Looe over the last few years.

Turning his thoughts back to the job in hand, Cowboy carried on looking. He wanted an outfit suitable for the Looe River View Hotel's cabaret night tonight.

"Why don't you go as a survivor from the 70's?" Keith had suggested "You won't have to dress any differently then" he'd added helpfully.

Cowboy was hoping he could find something that would make him look like Woody from Toy Story. His little grandson loved those films, and it would give grandad an opportunity to dress up regularly just like all his mates. He kept looking. Keith was now on the other side of the shop examining wedding dresses.

The numbers of people walking around the town reached a peak and by around 2pm, there wasn't a table to be had in any of the cafes, pubs or restaurants. The beach was busy too. The wind had dropped, and the bright sunshine had encouraged day trippers from nearby towns to add their numbers to the visitors from across the water in England. It wouldn't be long now until the first fight broke out in one of the pubs and Veryan and Lowenna's colleagues, would be making the first arrests of the weekend. This was usually the locals. They seemed to like putting on a show for the visitors. For the struggling business owners, it was embarrassing.

Easter Bank holiday weekends were always the worst. People would begin swigging on a Thursday evening and by Friday afternoon, quite often a jealous cousin or brother would be throwing punches at a former friend. "I've loved her all my life. She's my second cousin, we were supposed to get married" was heard more than once as lager overtook reason.

On the beach, Tony had come to Jesus's rescue. He'd been tied up for almost two hours and his previously pale skin was looking both scorched and slightly sand papered. Tony lent him a jacket and gave him some tea and after-sun in the seafront workshop before offering to drive him back through the street to his car.
Morley still had the crown of thorns on his head. It was properly wedged now and having peered at it in the tractor window, Morley realised he was probably going to have to drive to the minor injuries' unit in Liskeard in order to get it cut off. Tony offered to get the bolt cutters on it, but Morley declined. He was properly in character now, and he'd decided he was going to carry on being Jesus until he left town to go back to Bristol. He wasn't sure how he'd look with the thorns and the fluorescent hi-vis waterproof Tony had lent him, but he'd do his best.
Tony could hear a babble of voices outside the workshop, he went to have a look.

An excited crowd of about a hundred children was gathering around a man and donkey who were just about to descend the slope from the promenade down to the sand. Tony recognised Adi immediately. He was well known and well liked in the town. These days he didn't go out much and mostly occupied himself looking after his allotment and poly-tunnel next door to Emmety Villa.

 The signs said, 'No dogs on the beach', although Tony knew that legally, they were unenforceable. His employers had instructed him to encourage people not to take their dogs on the sand, and so reluctantly, he did his best to conform with their wishes. There wasn't anything about donkeys though.
He smiled at Adi as he caught his eye. "Hello mate, how are you? That's a rather unusual friend you've got there" Adi smiled back. "This is Ed" he gestured to his four-legged friend "The neighbours are strimming, and he gets agitated, I thought I'd bring him for a walk. He loves the beach."
Tony was a little surprised. He knew most things which went on in town and he certainly knew what went on around his beach. That Ed the donkey loved the beach was a revelation. "Oh, erm, do you bring him down here a lot then?" Adi smiled and nodded. "Yeah, most days, we come in the mornings mostly, don't we fella?" He gave the donkey an affectionate rub behind the ear.
The children, realising they weren't going to getting rides, began to disperse. Tony wasn't often lost for words, but this was going to take a few moments to compute. "Oh! How long has this been going on…..not that it's a problem

mate, after all, he's not a dog is he." Tony jerked a thumb at the sign. "Well," Adi replied "I've been looking after him for about six months now. Me and my neighbour rescued him, you remember Kirsten?"
Tony did remember her. She was known as the dolphin lady because of her involvement with Sea watch. "Rescued him, hmmm. Where was he before?"

Adi explained that Ed had appeared on nearby Seaton beach one day. One of the Sprygelly family has been dragging him up and down the beach in the baking sun all day, while relieving beachgoers of pound coins to carry their children up and down the hot sand. "And what they gave him for lunch was awful too" Adi explained. Tony inserted an "Oh?" in the correct place. "Yeah" Adi continued "Twenty minutes. Even my daughter got more than that when she worked down at the ice creamery. We couldn't let that carry on, so we bought him when the schools went back" Tony was intrigued. "Do you take him out very often?" "Oh yes" Adi replied, "We come down here every morning before everyone gets up and, in the evenings, we sometimes go for a wonder around the woods or up on the downs, we've even got him a high-vis jacket now, haven't we mate?" He rubbed Ed's ears again.

This was all brand-new information for Tony. "And he's happy, is he? I mean, not bothered by people or cars or anything?" "I think he quite likes people actually" Adi answered and then added "Except that prat Cowboy and his buddy Uncle Keith" Tony laughed. Those two both thought they were still 18 and the cocks of the town. They weren't 18, but the other part of the description fitted, just in a different manner form the way Uncle Keith and Cowboy thought of themselves. "Nice to see you mate, you must come up and see our poly-tunnel, we're doing really well now" Adi finished "Must get on, I promised him an ice cream" And with that, he led Ed down onto the sand and began to head towards the water so that they could both enjoy a paddle.

Veryan joined Lowenna back at the police station. There were three reports of erratic driving to follow up, all involving the same vehicle. Clearly something was amiss. All three drivers of the other cars had reported the same behaviour.
Apparently on the road between Looe and the dual carriageway, a brand-new silver BMW had been spotted driving behind the vehicles which had reported it.

The driver of the BMW had maintained a respectable distance from the car in front and at no point had it attempted to overtake. The driver had stayed within the speed limits even when coming into the 20-mph zone at the top of the town. It had also been observed that the driver had used the indicators of the BMW correctly at every junction. The driver had even put his hand up to thank the driver of a blue Peugeot van which had pulled over on a narrow stretch to let the BMW past.

Lowenna wondered if it was perhaps stolen, and the driver hadn't wanted to attract attention.
Veryan's response was that she thought the driver clearly hadn't read the owner's manual. They laughed as they climbed into the sergeant's patrol car to go and investigate.

On the way out of the small police car park, Lowenna noticed Cousin Morley's car still parked where he'd left it earlier in the day.
"Oh dear, I hope he's okay. All his clothes are still inside"
"I expect Ronnie or Reggie will let him in when they come on duty at two" Veryan answered. "Are you going to the

cabaret tonight Low? It's the fancy dress one."
Something which seemed to run in the family, indeed the town, was a love of fancy dress and dressing up. Lowenna had other plans for the evening though.
"The only thing I'll be dressing up in tonight are my slobs. It's going to be busy enough on Saturday and Sunday and we're both on early turn. Are you and Mike going then?" Veryan waved at a cousin as they drove along Station road.
"Yes, I think so. Mike didn't have a proper leaving do so the staff are getting together at the Looe View" she answered, shortening the name to the way the hotel was most referred to in the town. Then she added "I hear Jimmy has a new girlfriend"
Lowenna already knew.
"Yes, I saw them walking up to Emmety Villa earlier" She smiled knowingly. "Cousin Racheal, fancy that eh? She'll eat him alive"
They both laughed a long, knowing laugh.

It was a good day to be an estate agent in Looe. Peter hung up the phone. He had three offers on three apartments. In his profession, like a lot of other people in Looe, no one got paid anything extra for working on a Bank Holiday. The potential sale of three apartments had made the day a lot more worthwhile.

It helped that all three were going to be cash buyers. Hopefully, they could get past most of the stumbling blocks that other people encountered without too much difficulty.

Freehold flats were always a problem. Getting the owners of the freeholds to take care of their duties was almost always a major issue. Then there was the difficulty of getting mortgages on short lease properties; lenders were reluctant to take on anything with less than 80 years left on the lease. Then there were issues of restrictions. Time and again buyers had bought flats only to find that the leases forbade them from running an address as a business, and this included holiday letting. It was a minefield.

In the past, buyers from some backgrounds had been able to get around this, but recently The Special Club appeared to have lost a lot of influence in the town. Peter himself had witnessed a distinct drop in the numbers of Morning Dress-suited men with square briefcases walking through the town on the first Wednesday of every month. There had been a noticeable decrease in the number of phone calls he'd received instructing him on how things should be too.

Peter had never been a Special Club member, although he'd discussed it once with his cousin, Denzel. He did use the favour bank in the town though, and so sometimes favours had to be repaid. Peter preferred the way things were now. He hoped the sales would go through quickly. He had to deal with so many time wasters that three genuine buyers in a day was something to be celebrated.

He mused on the time wasters. Every day, people on holiday would gaze dreamily in through the windows of the agency and fantasise about living in the town. They'd come inside and make all the right noises, and then Peter and his team would waste hours traipsing around properties conducting viewings.
Once the viewers got home, they would realise that the complexities of moving were far too challenging, and then stop returning the agents phone calls. It was rude Peter thought, but it was also something he just had to grind his teeth to and put up with. Only one more summer though. Like so many other people working in the town, Peter had a plan.

Tonight, he was going to the cabaret, not as one of the guests, but as one of the performers. If his Frank Sinatra tribute act went down well, he was going to see if he could get some more bookings, and from then on, pointlessly herding Emmets around properties would be a thing of the past.

He thought about some of the places he'd been into in his eight years on the job. He'd seen some beautiful houses, and some absolute nightmares. You only had to spend ten minutes on Rightmove to see any number of decorating disasters. Then there were the 'enthusiasts', people who'd turned their houses into shrines for whatever their favourite thing was. There were the ones who adored Greek and Roman sculpture for instance. It was hard to explain to people why a one bedroomed former council flat, had faux marble columns stuck badly onto all the door frames. One two-bedroom flat in one block, had mounted two carved stone lions at the end of the 10-metre-long path. It was embarrassing.

Empty properties were easier to deal with, unless they were in what and he and his colleagues called the 'someone died' bracket. There was nothing wrong with the décor, some of the places were absolutes historical gems. Unfortunately, some of that history would have made a good backdrop to the type of plodding drama that Netflix showed about life in Russia in 1971, complete with stains.

The worst viewings were the places where the owners didn't have much awareness of hygiene. Peter cringed as he thought about some of those. If someone had accidentally left a dildo on display on a bedside table, Peter would do his best to obstruct the view with his body. That was a trivial thing though, some of the places were just plain foul. He shuddered when he recalled the Petri Dish cafes kitchen.
Peter clung to his dream like the survivor of a shipwreck would cling to a lifebuoy, and as he reminisced, he said a quick prayer that he could begin his new life as soon as possible.

As Peter reflected on his experiences, Jimmy was reflecting on his too. He'd learned quite a lot about Rachael in the last four hours, and although he was delighted at the beginning of their intimacy and losing his virginity, he was also in shock. Nothing he'd read in the staff room copies of Cosmopolitan and Take a Break, had prepared him for her enthusiasm. Rachael was clearly a lot more experienced than he was, and a lot more demanding. He was still shaking now as he walked back to his rented flat over the bookshop in the town centre. They planned to meet later once they'd bathed and dressed properly. Jimmy had to pick Rachael up at 7.30. Rachael had suggested he get some oysters and champagne for later. Although he was blissfully happy, Jimmy was completely out of his depth, and more than a little intimidated.

Jesus sat on the police station doorstep waiting for someone to let him in so he could retrieve his clothes and his car keys. The afternoon was becoming evening now and the last bit of warmth from the sun was ebbing away. Lowenna and Veryan had both gone off duty hours ago, and no one else had arrived. He didn't know that PC's Reginald and Ronald had been ordered to go to nearby Seaton where a shipping container had washed ashore, depositing hundreds of bottles of vodka into the sea and on to the beaches.

The coastguard was there too, but the sheer numbers of eager salvage hunters had overwhelmed them and all they could do was watch as excited members of the public filled their cars with the rare ocean bounty.

Clearly, he couldn't wait indefinitely shivering. Jesus was going to have to find somewhere to spend the evening and then collect his keys when Lowenna unlocked for early turn the following morning.

Cowboy and Uncle Keith couldn't believe their luck when one of the fishermen had walked into the pub and told the assembled drinkers about the scramble going on over at Seaton. They had a quick word with Rob, who they knew had a little half decker tied to the quay just a few hundred yards away.

Usually, he took people out fishing for mackerel and anything else which happened to swim by. This time they were going to go fishing, or more accurately, wading, for vodka.

All the fishermen knew to keep away from the Black Rock and particularly the section of coastline between Millendreath and Seaton. Rob however had spent years in those waters, and he knew how to get safely into the stretch known as Keveral Beach. There was almost a mile of beach here, access from either end was difficult and meant both scrambling over rocks and wading through several feet of water. The bounty hunters at Seaton would be going for the easy pickings. By navigating close enough to Keveral Beach, Rob, Keith and Cowboy would be able to retrieve far more working as a team than the other salvage hunters could collect in bags and holdalls, and they had the whole beach to themselves.

When they arrived, it looked as if an enormous shoal of bottles was bobbing about in the water. The sea was barely moving and so those bottles which arrived at the rocks took up temporary residence as the tide retreated, and more importantly, remained in most cases, intact.

Rob had to navigate carefully to avoid catching the remains of any of the floating cardboard boxes in the propeller of the little boat. Cowboy and Keith had squealed like excited children and had had to be restrained from jumping straight into the water while Rob found a safe place to temporarily anchor.

An hour after they'd arrived, the boat was full. Cowboy stayed on the beach while Rob and Keith sped across the water back to Looe. The quay was deserted as the pair unloaded into one of the fishermen's stores.

By the time they'd arrived back at Keveral Beach, Cowboy had had the foresight to gather as many bottles as he could and conceal them in a place well above the high tide mark. They could come back for them later.

Twice more the trio loaded the boat and then in a final effort, gathered as many of the floating bottles as they could, and concealed them well above the high-water mark. They could come back and retrieve them at the weekend.

Before that could happen, the fisherman's store had to be emptied, and discreetly at that.

Cowboy already had somewhere in mind for the precious salvage. He'd borrow his mate Stephens truck, go down to Cousin Denzel Sprygellys warehouse at the Millpool, and collect something to pack the bottles in. Denzel was in prison and several of his operations had ground to a halt recently. Cowboy didn't think anyone would notice if he hopped over the fence of the Looe water bottling plant and purloined a few hundred of the sparkling Looe water crates. Once the bottles had been rinsed off and packed, they could be taken up to the garages he was currently using as a tool store. While he did all the necessary work on Emmety Villa, no one would notice a few extra truckloads of deliveries.

Back in the present, the trio finished unloading. Cowboy pushed a bundle of twenties into Robs hand and said "Take a few bottles for yourself. Got to go now mate, me and Keith are heading for the cabaret tonight"

Rob had other plans. As Cowboy and Keith disappeared into the back streets, Rob took his boat out past the Banjo pier one more time and headed back towards Keveral Beach to do a spot of 'fishing' for himself.

As evening approached, a predictable scene began to emerge. Families shuffled from one eating establishment to another trying to find one with a vacant table. The bakeries sold their last few pasties and the fish and chip shops dished up hundreds of portions to ravenous Emmets. In the small supermarket, fridges, shelves and freezers were stripped of anything which might be considered suitable for a barbecue. The disappointed late comers would have to be content with pizzas and crisps.

Rubbish bins over-flowed and thoughtless people blocked the flow of traffic while they waited for their partners to 'just nip in' to one of the take-aways or shops. It never occurred to them that the rules on traffic and parking included them too.
Sunburnt, over tired, sugar filled toddlers, grizzled in their pushchairs while their parents sought out places for a few beers before they got taxis back to whichever of the many caravan parks they were staying at.

The sensible ones had booked tables or done their shopping early. The remainder, a considerable proportion, were willing to take their chances, and were beginning to discover what a poor choice that had been. The mood in the town was impatient and tetchy.

In his tiny office in the small supermarket, Dermot kept his head down as the staff attempted to deal with the onslaught.
Dermot wasn't just out of his depth, he was undeniably drowning.

He'd tried ringing Jimmy to get him to come in, but Jimmy, unusually, wasn't answering his phone.

Dermot could have gone home himself, but he lacked the courage to walk past his staff on his way to the door, knowing that he was abandoning them to the horrors of the mob.

He locked himself inside his tiny cubicle and hoped his staff would think he'd already left. He had a four pack of Rattler to keep him company. He began soothing his troubles in earnest.

Dotted around the residential areas of the town, an assortment of items of fancy dress were being put on. The Looe River View Easter Cabaret was an occasion people marked on their calendar's months in advance. The fire certificate said 300 people maximum in the function room, but everyone knew that at least double that could fit in, and regularly did.

The theme this year was Easter. It made sense and still offered plenty of variety. Not everyone would stick to the suggestion though, and it made for a colourful, if at times, confusing evening.

In the middle flat in Emmety Villa, Alan Higginbottom had put the wizard outfit back on. He and his mate The Salmon, were enjoying a few glasses of Thunderbird prior to heading out.

In the hotel, Norman and Marjorie were trying on the outfits they'd brought with them for the second time that afternoon. Norman had picked an outfit designed to make him look like a fried egg. Marjorie had wanted to be the Easter Bunny, but what had arrived was a Bunny Girl outfit.

The effect of Norman had been remarkable.

If only Norman hadn't got cramp at a crucial moment, and Marjorie's knees not been so creaky, and Normans back almost popped a disc mid-passion, it would have been perfect.

Marjorie watched the fires in Normans eyes reignite as she fastened her bunny ears for the second time. She'd planned to give the outfit away after this evening, but now, it looked as if there was some potential in keeping it.

Donald and Sylvia were saving their passion for later. Sylvia knew just the right amount of real ale to feed to Donald to inspire his ardour. He'd confided in her about the pills too, and so they'd arrange that he'd take one at around 10pm. Donald had decided to go as one of the 12 disciples. This was as close to religion as he'd ever been, except getting religiously plastered whenever the rugby was on.

Sylvia had found an outfit called 'The Easter Chick'. It had been ordered over the internet, and Sylvia could see it probably wasn't well enough stitched to last very long. Sylvia was wishing she'd chosen something different, but it was too late now, so as she pulled on her yellow tights, she resigned herself to having a few cocktails and doing her best to enjoy the evening. Anyway, they were celebrating. This would be the last time they stayed in Looe as visitors, soon, like their new friends Norman and Marjorie, they would be residents.

Paul Sprygelly did his best to flit between the busy bar and the reception desk. The place was rapidly filling up, and it was only 7.45, the show wasn't due to begin until 9pm. He mentally reviewed the itinerary.

At 9pm, the proceeding would be opened by local celebrity and Pauls third cousin twice removed on his father's side, Rachael DeSprygelly. Lenny the Lugworm would then welcome everyone, tell a few scripted jokes and introduce the first act. Local Duo, Phil & Doreen would sing a few folk songs. Next up was Frank Sinatra. After that was John the plumber who was going to have his first go at stand-up comedy. Lastly, the amazing Louise and her snake were due to captivate the assembled crowd. Everyone had 15 minutes.

While all this was going on, most of the audience would be seated, and a small buffet in the ticket holder's area would be laid out.

There would be a half hour break, mainly to encourage people to spend money at the bar, and then the grand finale would be an hour extravaganza of songs from Boney M-ish, the only tribute band he'd been able to get at short notice, when Who-ever, the Who tribute band, had cancelled last weekend.

After that, the disco would play until 11.45, by which time most of the oldies would have shuffled off to bed. The locals would chant 'more' for five minutes knowing that the disco would then go on until 3am.

In the small corridor behind the stage, Leonard finished his pint and pulled on the headpiece before coming out onto the floor to mingle and begin to get the audience warmed up.

The display of outfits was dazzling. There were several Easter Bunnies and Bunny girls, Jesus was there, in fact five Jesuses in all. There were also numerous attempts at disciples, Mary mother of Jesus was also well represented. Leonard recognised Alan Higginbottom; he was in that wizard outfit again. Locals were starting to refer to him as the Emmety Villa wizard all the time now, or sometimes, Alan the wizard. There was his mate 'The Salmon too. Leonard watched as the giant fish took a mouthful of Guinness. It was slightly surreal.

Paul was observing the crowd from behind the bar as he tried to keep up with the demand for drinks. A party of Smurfs was just coming in. No doubt everything would be covered in blue chalk paint later. Paul wandered if they were the same group as last year. He hoped not. There had been trouble between the Smurfs and a group of Oompah Loompas, several cheese footballs had been used as projectiles. It had all been thoroughly disagreeable, especially when he'd had to ask members of both groups to leave. The ensuing brawl on the quayside had garnered more attention that the Cabaret, but at least it had happened outside. Paul reassured himself. There were plenty of staff on this evening, and the crowd was either easily recognisable locals or elderly members of the coach party. What could possibly go wrong?

Woody from Toy Story and Little Bo Peep presented themselves at the bar.

"Evening Cowboy, good evening Keith, have you paid for your tickets yet" Paul asked knowing full well the pair had just come through the kitchen fire door. He didn't give them time to answer.

"Three pounds each gentlemen, or should I say, Lady and gentleman" and he held out two stamped rubber wristbands.

Bo Peep gave Paul a beaming smile, Cowboy huffed loudly as he pulled out his wallet.

Lenny the Lugworm climbed on stage and allowed the last few stragglers to come through from the bar into the function room. The lights were dimmed, the small band gave a drum roll, and Lenny began his routine.

At the back of the room Bo Peep spoke quietly to Cowboy 'Come on then, give us a couple' Woody dipped into his waistcoat and took out four tablets, two diamond shaped blue ones, and two white ones with what looked like a picture of a pigeon on them. "Down the hatch" he said passing one of each to Bo Peep as he placed the other two onto his tongue, took a swig of lager, and tipped his head backwards.

"How many did you bring?" Keith asked his accomplice.

"Ten of each, plus one of each for us. Which ones do you want to try with?"

"I'll try flogging the white ones if that's alright mate, I think they're Ecstasy tablets."

"Righto, then these ought to be them Niagara's" Cowboy answered. Three pound a pop yeah? And we'll see what happens."

Donald and Sylvia sat with Norman and Marjorie on a table just to the right of the stage. As the lights went down, Marjorie reached into her bag and quickly filled everyone's glasses with Malibu. Elsewhere in the room, other canny oldies were topping up glasses too. It might well be discount drinks, but who wanted to have to keep going to the bar?

Marjorie looked over to the adjacent table. One of the men sitting there was pouring a thick white goo into a wine glass from what looked like a medicine bottle. The man caught Marjorie looking at him and whispered "Anti indigestion liquid, it's to pave the way for the Pernod" he indicated a bottle sticking out of his wife's handbag. Marjorie winked at him approvingly.

Lenny was on joke number four; many of the older visitors had made the most of free sherry in the bar at 6pm followed by complimentary glasses of punch from 7pm until 8pm. They were already well lubricated and laughed appreciatively at jokes which had been around for as long as they had.

Jesus had given up waiting at the police station and had been going from Bed and breakfast to Hotel only to find everywhere so far was fully booked.

On the road outside the Looe River View, his bare foot trod on a screw which had been carelessly dropped in the road. He bent to pick it up and as he reached for it, spotted another one, and then another. Soon he had eight screws. He remembered that the hotel he was standing outside had staff quarters, so perhaps he might just be able to find a bed for the night in here.

Jesus walked up the steps and in through the main doors. Paul was back on reception now and he smiled at Jesus as he approached, recognising him from his time in Looe before he'd gone up north. Paul suspected they were probably cousins.
Jesus put the eight screws on the desk and spoke.
"I found them lying in the road outside. I don't suppose you could put me up for the night?"

Paul somehow, managed to retain his composure, and answered "We have a small room at the back, it's the night porters rest room, it's a bit cave like and the door is heavy, would that be okay for now?"

"That would be fine" answered Jesus, and at that point Morley decided he no longer had to maintain his performance. "In't you cousin Poppy's boy? Poppy Butters?"
"I am, Morley. That thing on your head looks painful, would you like to come through to the kitchen and we'll see if we can get it off?"
Morley gratefully acquiesced and allowed himself to be led through the rear door to a quiet corner of the catering area. While the crowd sang along to 'All around my hat' in the function room, Paul and Leonard set about removing the embedded crown of blackthorn spikes with a pair of meat scissors and a pair of pliers.

Cowboy decided the best place to make a sale was inside the gents' toilet. There was a machine on the wall that offered condoms and fake Viagra. It meant lurking in a suspicious manner for a while, but Cowboy had been practicing that all his life. It wasn't long before Donald came in to relieve himself. Sherry, punch and malibu had given him a rosy glow and he was feeling kindly disposed towards the world.

He rinsed his hands and as he wafted them around under the wheezy hand drier, proceeded to study the machine. This was Cowboy's cue.

"I've got something far more potent than those if you're interested?"

Donald, accustomed to doing deals for weed and pills in toilets was unsurprised and unfazed.

"Really? The real deal?"

"22 Caret, proper job lady pleasers they are, three pounds each if you want a couple?"

Donald couldn't believe his ears. He was used to paying far more. He fished in his pocket for his wallet.

"I'll have thirty" he answered without hesitation.

Cowboy was astounded. "I've only got ten on me, but if you wait a while, I can come back with another twenty?"

Donald nodded. "How about thirty quid for the ten you've got now, and I'll give you another fifty quid for the other twenty when you come back.

Cowboy, never the sharpest knife in the box queried the amount "That's sixty mate, not fifty"

"How about a little discount for a bulk purchase?" Donald replied.

"Oh, yeah, sure, okay then"

Donald handed over three ten-pound notes, Cowboy handed back the little bag of pills which Donald immediately stuffed into the pocket of his biblical robe.

The door of the toilet opened, and The Salmon took a pace inside, realised he was interrupting something, muttered a quick "I'll come back later" and stepped back out again. "I'm on a table at the front, come and find me when you have the rest" Donald said.
Cowboy nodded his head enthusiastically. He'd just made twenty pounds, if he could get the other fifty, he'd have made almost the same amount as he would probably spend on lager this evening. Things were looking encouraging.

He felt a surge of energy fill his body, the room seemed to pulse with fluorescence, and he felt a wonderful feeling of peace overcome his entire being. He leaned forward and clasped Norman in a strong embrace. "I'll see you soon, I love you man!" and then he released the rather taken aback Donald, turned around, and exited the lavatory. As he made his way back to the function room, the music was so lovely, he could almost see the notes wafting along the corridor. Phil & Doreen were singing 'Cousin Jack'. It had never sounded so beautiful. As the white tablet coursed through his system, Cowboy loved everybody, man.

Morley explained what had happened as Paul bandaged his head. In the morning he'd be able to get his wallet back, and his clothes. He'd settle the bill and head back to Bristol. Paul was fine with this; Morley was family after all. Paul asked Morley if he knew who was on duty this evening. He'd probably have their phone number. Morley didn't know but suggested that Cousin Lowenna probably would. Paul knew better than to ring Lowenna out of working hours. He said he'd leave a message on the stations answerphone just in case anyone happened to see it flashing later.

Next came something to eat, Leonard filled a plate with a selection from the platters laid out for the buffet. Morley gulped it down and then emptied a second plate.
Paul looked on and mentally made a note of Jesus being catered to by the Lugworm. If he ever wrote a book about his experiences, that was definitely going in it.

"Thanks fella, I'll see you in the morning" Morley thanked Paul as he showed him to the small cupboard containing the zedbed that the night staff sometimes used. The exhausted and grateful Morley was asleep in minutes. For the rest of the evening, various staff members paused outside the door to snigger. Morley's snoring sounded like a whoopee cushion.

Back at the police Station, late turn had arrived for the pre-shift-change briefing. There was nothing out of the ordinary other than the report about thousands of bottles of vodka being washed up along a six mile stretch of coastline. One of the PC's found the note that Morley had left on the back door on paper he'd scrounged at the petrol station next door.

The note explained that his belongings were inside and that he'd be back in the morning. Luckily, when Paul rang the police station, PC Martin Sprygelly, was the one to answer. He soon established what had happened.

"No problem" he told his cousin "We'll bring his gear over in about ten minutes"

After a harrowing Friday with truly little Good about it, Jesuses suffering was coming to an end.

Inside the function room, both Woody and Bo Peep were dancing. They were the only ones on their feet, and no one had ever seen two old men dancing to 'Michael rowed the boat ashore.' It was quite a spectacle. The fact that Bo Peep was sporting an obvious erection beneath his frock, just added to the voyeuristic horror of the onlookers. Woody and Bo Peep were oblivious. The vibes man, they were so cool.

Woody had a similar biological response and he realised to his horror that he really shouldn't have taken both pills, rather just the white one.

"I hope it stops soon" Cowboy leaned towards Keith "I can't stop dancing if they don't stop playing"

"I know mate, I love you man" Keith tried to hug Cowboy, Cowboy pushed him away.

"I love you too man, but don't do that eh? Especially not while you got your fishing rod up"

"Sorry dude" Bo Peep fluttered her long false eyelashes.

At last, the song came to an end. "I've got to nip home. I'll be about 20 minutes" Cowboy told the over affectionate Keith.

"No worries, I'll be here on the dance floor" Keith answered. There was no way he was leaving yet; he was just beginning to find his groove. Phil played the opening notes of Agadoo. "Oh mate, I love this" he continued, but

Cowboy was already on his way before he got trapped on the dancefloor for the whole night. He had money to make, and he urgently needed to visit Charity Sally in her little flat overlooking the bridge. He whispered a silent prayer that she wasn't offering her charity to anyone else this evening.

Keith decided he'd give Cowboys approach a go. He rapidly discovered that wearing his Bo Peep outfit in the gents and suggesting to an assortment of men that he could help them 'have a good time' for three pounds, attracted more animosity than customers. The sixth person to enter the toilet was Norman. Keith decided to adopt a different approach.
"Good tonight don't you think" he offered to Norman while pretending to wash his hands.
Norman was busy trying to find the zipper somewhere in his egg white.
Norman zipped himself up. "Well, it's different from the concerts I used to go to, but the wives are enjoying it"
Keith took the cue. "Oh yeah, who did you used to go and see?" he was delighted when Norman answered.
"Oh you know, Primal Scream, Happy Mondays, a few others"
Keith didn't bother protracting the conversation, he knew if he stayed in there much longer one of the earlier bunch would be back, and that might mean that punches were thrown.
"I've got some dancing tablets if you know what I mean? Just like the raves in the late eighties"
Norman was interested. "How much?"
"Three pound each"
"How about four for ten?" Norman haggled.
Keith was desperate to take some money following Cowboy's success. "Okay then" and he extended his hand

to accept the note Norman had already taken out of his pocket.

There was a fumble as Keith dipped into the Bo Peep handbag and handed four white pigeon pills to Norman.

"Plenty more if you need 'em"

Norman paused "Oh, are they no good then?"

"Oh no mate, they're fine, just offering"

"Hmmm" Norman turned his back on the drug dealer and went back to his table.

"I'm going to the bar" he announced raising his left thumb and scratching his right ear, "Donald, would you mind giving me a hand?" Donald smiled and rose to his feet. "Certainly" and he began scratching his right ear with his left thumb, which in Special Club code meant, I've got something I want to say to you in private, back.

Away from the ears of their wives, Norman was first. "I got four ecstasy tablets from Bo Peep." At first Donald wondered if there was some code being spoken that he couldn't recall. Then he remembered the spectacle of Bo Peep and the Toy story character embarrassing themselves with their arthritic stumbling attempts to dance.

They leaned on the edge of the bar facing one another. "Oh, Jolly good. The Cowboy one sold me some Viagra. He's just gone to get some more, would you like some?"

Norman nodded to indicate that yes he would.

The barman asked for the second time "What can I get you gents?"

"Oh, how many, and how much?"

Donald explained and then finished by saying, I wonder if he's got any more of the whiteys? Marjorie and I used to stay up all night when Eurovision was on. We'd watch it live, and then watch the recording straight after. It was great"

The barman asked again.

"Gent's, were you waiting to be served?"

The new friends were lost in a reverie of their excesses four decades previously.

The barman gave up trying to get their attention and went to serve someone else.

Lenny the Lugworm and Rachael De Sprygelly exchanged banter on stage while the hotel staff engaged in a frantic search of the behind-the-scenes areas. Lenny was almost out of material and he was silently praying that Rachael would be able to keep going in pleasing the audience while his colleagues tried to locate the missing eight-foot python.

The amazing Louise hopped anxiously from foot to foot and swore under her breath.
"Bloody thing, I knew we were both getting far too old for this. I bet the little sod has found the boiler room, wherever that is"
Charlie, the python, had obviously been hungry. There was clear evidence he'd found the trollies of platters which had been intended for the buffet.
In the kitchen, Paul and the chef were hurriedly piping a fresh batch of shrimp paste into a mountain of vol au vents.
The slippery git had probably tucked himself away somewhere warm while he slept off his meal. Louise hoped he wouldn't be too lethargic when he was found. He was much harder to dance with when he was dopey.
She checked her make up again in the mirror by the kitchen door. For 64 years old, she thought she still looked hot in her little silver bikini. Most of the male members of staff did their best not to stare. Fortunately, Louise hadn't heard when one of the waiters had quipped "Oh she's okay, she just needs ironing" when she'd come to inform Paul of the absent reptile.

A celebratory shout announced Charlie had been found tucked in behind a row of deep fat fryers.
Louise checked her hair again and went to retrieve her dozy co-performer.

In the cabaret room, Jimmy applauded loudly as his beloved Rachael told another knock knock joke. He thought to himself that she could be quite funny sometimes, for a girl. Considering that his own brand of humour consisted mostly of dad jokes, they made a splendid pair.
Most of the rest of the audience groaned and clapped half-heartedly as Rachael did her best to fill the space where Louise and Charlie should have been right now.
The only table that was really going for it was the table with the fried egg and the bunny girl, the disciple and the, whatever the big yellow ball of fluff was supposed to be. There was no stopping that lot, they were like a group of Young Farmers at a Wurzels gig. They were giving it everything.

At last Louise and Charlie appeared at the edge of the performers area. A greatly relieved Rachael introduced them and quickly exited the stage to take up her seat next to Jimmy again. He was sitting down talking to his former colleague Mike, and Veryan who were both dressed as crucifixes.
"You were wonderful" he said as he clasped her hand firmly and looked deeply into her eyes. Everyone else in the room was looking at the stage in voyeuristic fascination as the music for Michael Jacksons Thriller started. Louise began what looked like a series of physiotherapy exercises while wiggling the comatose reptile at the horrified onlookers.
As Louise finished her performance and accepted the applause of the confused audience, Cowboy reappeared in the room.
He narrowly avoided a collision with a service trolly as the staff began to load up the allocated tables with the buffet

platters. He grabbed a handful of cheese and pineapple on sticks as another trolly whooshed past.

Keith had spotted him and so he made his way across the room to intercept him.
Cowboy was wide eyed and looked rather worried.
"Have you got any pills left?" He gasped to Bo Peep.
Keith stopped to adjust his stocking before answering. "I sold four, I've still got the rest"
"Well get rid of them quick, there was a copper standing in reception when I came in"
"Bugger" Keith exclaimed. He couldn't afford to get caught with anything, not again. He shot an angry look at the table where the bloke who'd bought the four pills was. It must have been them who called the Old Bill. Looking at them though, it was quite clear that all four were currently high as kites, so perhaps not. Still, he couldn't take any chances. He quickly pulled the little bag with the remaining pills from his handbag.

Paul Sprygelly walked across the room with the uniformed constable and went out through the rear door to return Morley's bag of belongings.
Keith was beginning to panic now. "What the 'ell shall I do wiv 'em?"
Cowboy, a veteran at escaping tricky situations, plucked a vol au vent from one of the platters and thrust it towards Keith. "Use these, I'll get some more"
While the attention in the room was still focussed on Louise and Charlie, six vol au vents had six ecstasy tablets inserted into them, and then were swiftly returned to the buffet table.

"What about the rest that you've got?" Keith asked

Cowboy.

"I didn't make it home" Cowboy confessed. "I got to Sally's and completely forgot what I'd gone out for."

"Let's get a drink" Keith suggested "I love you man" Cowboy was a little more relaxed again now and he felt another rush as the drugs he'd consumed pulsed around his head.

Offering his arm to Bo Peep, he answered, "I love you too man" and the pair left the buffet to head out to the reception area bar.

Rachael, never one to waste the offer of free food, led Jimmy to the buffet and began loading a plate before the old vultures, as she thought of them, had a chance to strip the table bare. There were many mutterings in the queue behind her as she piled crab sticks and cheese straws onto her plate.
"Vol-au vent?" Jimmy suggested indicating the plate.
"Go on then, just the one" Jimmy passed one to her. Her plate was so full he had to stand it on top of the Quiche Lorraine. He put one on his own plate while he was there.

Donald and Sylvia were on the dance floor doing their finest John Travolta and Olivia Newton John impressions. Unfortunately, the music they were dancing to was Queen and David Bowies Under Pressure. The ghost of Freddie Mercury looked on flabbergasted. Freddie liked to visit Looe a lot. It was his kind of town. Sometimes though he ended up regretting some of the sights he witnessed. Now was one. "Dave, Dave?" he called out through the ether, "Come and have a look at this" The ghost of David Bowie reluctantly pulled himself away from the filming of a night scene for Coronation Street. David loved his soaps. He was rather alarmed to see Donald and Sylvias gyrations.
"They'd better go steady, one of them is bound to pop a hip if they keep that up"
Freddie nodded in agreement. "Have you ever seen such a thing?"
David cupped his chin for a moment as he gave the matter some thought. "Not since that time Elton and Cliff tried to make that bloody awful Christmas record" he responded. "Do you remember?"
Freddie did remember, and he quietly thanked every DJ everywhere for refusing to ever give it any airtime.

The two ghosts decided to hang around and see what else would happen that night.

On the other side of the river, East Looe buzzed with activity too. Fast food outlets maintained a brisk pace while shunting out food to hungry families. The bars were full, so were the restaurants. Taxis barely stopped at the rank before another group of sweaty, boozy hopefuls descended on them. The taxi drivers remained calm as they ferried their loads around. They patiently drove while having the same predictable conversations they would have to endure every night for months now.

The little supermarket was closed. From the safety of his office, Dermot had heard the last cashier lock the till drawers in the safe in the adjacent room.
There would be no night fill this evening. Dave, David and Davey had all rung in and left messages on the answerphone to say they were poorly. If Dermot had been a little more aware, he'd have realised that the trio were elsewhere with most of the other staff members celebrating Mike's liberation and weren't poorly at all. Indeed, the trio of Mariachi who were currently loading sausages on sticks and vol au vents onto plates just over the river looked to be in excellent health.

In the morning, Dermot was going to have a lot on his plate. Jimmy usually came in early and made sure everything was ready for opening. Jimmy had booked the morning off months ago and had staunchly refused to budge.
As in many supermarkets, Jimmy was a member of staff who constantly worked ten or even twenty hours over the forty he was paid for. It had been a regular, abusive practice which had gone on since at least the 1970's. It still went on in supermarkets across the country even today.
Dermot had had no option other than to say he would fill

in for Jimmy just this once.

If Dermot had been possessed of any integrity, he'd have told his bosses they needed to inject some more hours into the shop, after all, they took enough profit out of it. Sadly, as Employment Compliance Officer Mark Wray understood only too well in *his* job, integrity was a rare commodity.

Dermot knew there would be deliveries during the small hours. Bread, milk and newspapers would all have to be unloaded, taken in and delivery notes checked. He was going to have a busy night. He unlocked his office and headed quickly up the stairs to use the smelly lavatory. Someone ought to clean that he thought. It didn't occur to him that it was his responsibility.
Afterwards, for the first time in hours, he walked onto the shop floor. He made a quick assessment of what needed to be done. In short, everything. He helped himself to another 4 pack of Rattler. He reckoned the company could afford it. He certainly wasn't going to get paid for the extra hours. It was notable that he could apply that thinking to himself, but not to the staff in his charge.

He opened a can and began loading boxes of biscuits onto a trolly in the storeroom. The whole shop had looked as if the population had been apocalypse shopping. Without his key players, Dermot knew he'd barely make a dent in the work that needed to be done, but for once, to his credit, he was going to try.
He took a long pull of Rattler. His ears didn't register the footsteps on the metal staircase leading to the flats upstairs. In the meantime, as Dermot moved the biscuits, Rob was

busy outside transporting a satisfying 160 bottles of vodka from his boat up to the safety of his apartment.

Boney M-ish were rocking the room, although it was noticeable that some people were rocking more than others.
Twelve of them to be precise.
The four at the front had been straight on their feet when the band had opened with 'The rivers of Babylon'. Rachael and Jimmy had been up too, much to Jimmy's surprise, he'd never danced in public in his life. Jimmy was feeling good, and everything around him seemed to be glowing, he decided it must have been the cocktails.
Woody from Toy Story and Bo Peep were grooving too, as were the trio of Mariachi. The last person, who had hungrily eaten the last vol au vent when the virtually empty platters were being brought back into the kitchen, was Paul Sprygelly.
Paul was feeling good, in fact he was feeling better than good, he could feel the love in the room, almost as if it were cotton wool.

The opening bars of 'Daddy Cool' played and a few more of the audience decided to join the dancing. If Bo Peep and the day manager were making exhibitions of themselves, then everyone else might as well join in.
The arthritic performance which ensued made the amazing Louise look as fluid as the original dancers from the original band.

Fuelled by complimentary cocktails, Cherry B's and pints of Atlantic light ale, the audience in the Looe River View hotel partied like it was 1999.
Even Alan the Wizard and WPC Veryan joined in.

The Ghosts of Freddie and David looked on. "Well, that didn't turn out so badly after all, did it Dave?"

Mr Bowie smiled back at his friend "Indeed it didn't, shall we dance?"
Unnoticed by almost everyone, they made their way to the front of the room and joined in with the dancers.

Paul carried on dancing at the end of the bar and as the amused chef went past said to him "Look at that, we've even got a Freddie Mercury and a David Bowie in tonight, wow they look great don't they"

Woody leaned towards Bo Peep "Look at Paul. I saw him take a vol au vent, I reckon he must have had one."
Bo Peep nodded back "Well at least now we know they work"
Woody and Bo Peep congratulated themselves on their cleverness. They had no idea of the come down they were hurtling toward.

The band played on mixing covers from other artists in with their own brand of funky and Boney m's original hits. They ended with Rasputin which finished to a rapturous applause.
The crowd wasn't ready to let them go, and both Paul and Rachael climbed on stage to encourage them to play an encore.
They had to play Rasputin four more times until the crowd was satisfied.

Saturday morning was considerably less pleasurable than the previous evening.

Jimmy was woken by an insistent pounding on his door. He untangled himself from Rachael and staggered to snatch a dressing gown before stumbling out into the hallway. He paused briefly as he recalled the previous evening. What a night. They'd danced, they'd sung, they'd had a good chat with a couple of blokes dressed like David Bowie and Freddie Mercury, and then they'd come home.

Jimmy and Rachael had found themselves engaged in a passion so hot it almost scorched the wallpaper.

Another crescendo of knocks brought his attention back to the pounding on his door.
Jimmy opened it to find a now uniformed Veryan standing on the doorstep.
"Hi Jimmy, sorry to bother you, especially after last night, but all the staff are on the doorstep of the shop and there's no one around who has any keys"
"What time is it?" Jimmy answered "It was fun wasn't it? I hope Mikes not got a hangover"
"Mikes fine" she smiled "I'm amazed you're looking so" she paused "radiant" Veryan checked her watch and continued "It's quarter past nine"
Jimmy took a sharp intake of breath and an abrupt step backwards.
"Oh my God. Is Mark there? Is Joyce?"
"Yes, they're all waiting. If you can let me have the keys, I'll take them down."
Jimmy nodded and without bothering to respond, began rummaging in the pocket of his jacket which was hanging up just inside the door. He retrieved a hefty bunch of keys

and thrust them towards his cousin.

"I'll get dressed; I'll be there as quick as I can. Oh my God, we should have been open at 7.30"

"Thanks Jimmy, see you later love" Veryan took the keys and wasted no time in making her way back down the stairs.

Jimmy closed the door and walked back through to his sitting room where he plonked himself down on the sofa. For absolutely no reason he could fathom, he burst into tears.

Rachael was woken by the sound of Jimmy's sobbing. She was confused. She went through to join him and sat down beside him while offering a comforting arm around his shoulders, whereupon, for no reason she could fathom, she burst into tears too.

Breakfast in the Looe River view Hotel had barely been attended. This was hardly surprising as many of the visiting coach party had still been dancing at 3am.

Paul was relieved. He'd managed to get a couple of hours sleep in the office. He always kept a fresh set of clothes at work, so he'd showered in the staff bathroom. That, along with numerous cups of coffee hadn't done much to revive him. The whole world felt fuzzy. Not like that lovely feeling from the night before, this felt as if the sky were about to collapse. He had a horrible feeling in his stomach that something really bad was about to happen.

It was the staff and owners meeting later. Paul felt an icy hand wrap around him.

The coaches were parked outside preparing to take the last party of visitors back to their homes.

Zombie like guests shuffled into the reception area hauling

bags laden with sachets of marmalade, everlasting muffins, and a cornucopia of fridge magnets.

Donald and Sylvia could barely walk. Donald walked crab like clutching the walls as he tried to get his hips and knees to cooperate.

"I think we over did it a bit" Sylvia offered "Do you think the driver will mind grabbing our cases, I don't think I could have managed one of them this morning, let alone four"

"I've got twenty pounds for him if he will" Donald answered before continuing "Lummy, I wish I had some codeine, my head feels okay but my back is killing me"

In their room, Norman and Marjorie were experiencing similar discomforts, but with the accompaniment of the come-down that hadn't yet caught up with Donald and Sylvia.

Unlike Jimmy and Rachael, the couple knew where their bluesy feelings were coming from.

"Never ever again!" Marjorie told her husband. "I know it was fun last night, but I haven't felt this lousy since the last time we went to Glastonbury."

"I know" Norman echoed sympathetically "I hope to hell I don't start crying, it was bad enough that time I had the come down and The Littlest Hobo was on the telly. I couldn't stop weeping at the theme tune"

"We had better get moving or we're going to miss the bus. I can't carry all this lot; do you think we should leave some of the muffins?"

Norman agreed that they could, and they began to decant one of their cases into the drawers of the bedside cabinets.

Cowboy and Keith hadn't stopped. They were still dressed in their outfits. They were puffing and panting as the lugged boxes of vodka bottles up the steps to the sheds at Emmety Villa.

Alan had heard them moving around outside at 5am and had gone to have a look at from his kitchen window. More weirdness. Such was life at Emmety Villa. He had picked up the wizard's hat from the sofa and stroked it affectionately before going back to bed.

It was almost 10am now and Cowboy and Keith were still carrying boxes up.
Keith had started to cry, and Cowboy was comforting him while holding back his own tears. At least the 'Niagara's' had worn off he thought to himself, that had been excruciating. He wouldn't be doing that again.

Cowboy was experiencing the same feeling of dread as Paul. He wanted to get finished, he needed some alone time, and preferably some sleep.

The three Mexicans were doing marginally better. At the end of the disco, they'd gone from the Looe River View with Mike and Veryan, plus a few of Mikes other former colleagues, to Mikes new shop.
Veryan had said goodnight and gone straight to the station to get her head down in a cell before going on shift at 6am.

In the storeroom and office at Mikes, with an abundance of good Cornish wine and beer at their disposal, the Mariachi and the other supermarket staff had carried on with their party. Mike had already decided not to open again until Monday. The party was still going at 7am.
Dave, David and Davey would experience their come down horrors later.

At last, the coach pulled away and Paul went back inside to his office. He had ten minutes before the meeting with Mark Wray and the hotel owners was due to begin.
Still with a sense of impending doom, he reached for the phone which was ringing with a call direct to his personal line.
He was horrified to hear a familiar voice on the end of the line.

"Hi Paul, it's your cousin, Denzel. I wonder if you could give me a lift next Friday"

# Summer.

Alan Higginbottom watched from his window as the Man and Van which had brought Jimmy's belongings, pulled away.
A lot had happened in the last few weeks. Alan and Eileen had new neighbours in three apartments. They all seemed nice, but Alan was a little unsettled when both men from downstairs had returned his handshake with a clasp he instantly recognised as Special Club member identification. Alan didn't want anything to do with the Special Club.

Alan and Eileen's cousin, the notorious Denzel was back in town. He was a special Club member too. Thankfully in the weeks since his return, Denzel hadn't contacted them. From the snippets of information Alan and Eileen had gleaned, Cousin Denzel was doing his utmost to become a committee member for the Town Welcome and Tourist Support. Eileen had commented when she'd shared the news "He's certainly got the pedigree for it"

Alan turned his attention back to the task he'd been avoiding, looking for a new job. In a few short weeks, Alan would be 55. Like so many others in the town, he'd done a wide variety of jobs over the years as one type of employment dried up and another began. He'd worked at the towns small garden centre for nineteen years now. The garden centre had just been sold though, and the new owner, whether legal or not, intended to fire all the existing staff and replace them with people of his own choosing.

This would be a great blow to the town. Alan was well known, well liked, and he'd done his job exceptionally well.

Later, when the garden centre went bust, the new owner would regret his decisions and Alan and Eileen would lament the loss of another thriving business, but no one could see that particular future now, otherwise Alan might have looked to start a similar business himself.

Alan did have another job. Almost everyone who lived in the town did; they had to in order to survive the winters. Alan worked as a handyman. Self-employment was all well and good he knew, but there was nothing like the safety net of having an employer, or so he'd thought until the garden centre had been sold.
What was he going to do? He looked at his feet. He was wearing the wizard's slippers. Eileen had accepted his new passion now and she was even beginning to embrace it herself. They had an alter now and they'd begun performing rituals under the full moon at the top of the garden. There was even some evidence to suggest that the rituals were beginning to work. They'd won ten pounds on lucky dips from the lottery, four times in the last three months. The magic *must* be working.

He sat down at his computer and half-heartedly continued to look through the listings for jobs.
Parking attendant, Tree surgeon, Waiter, Care assistant and more in a similar vein. Alan shuddered when he spotted vacancies that were clearly for some of Cousin Denzel's businesses. There was nothing listed that he couldn't do, but his heart sank at the thought of most of them. He carried on looking through the lists and extended the search area.
Fancy dress shop manager. Now there was one he could easily manage, and it looked enjoyable. Oh, it was in St Ives at the far end of the county. That was too far for Alan, but

he smiled broadly to himself as an idea began to form. He opened a new window on screen and began to search Copywriting and Trademarks. Alan had a new plan. It was almost midsummers day, a good time to do some more magic he decided. He wriggled his toes contentedly in his wizard's slippers.

Denzel Sprygelly was as loud and obnoxious as he'd been before he'd gone to prison. Everyone knew where he'd been, and no one said a word. Denzel himself referred to his absence as his 'little holiday'.
His banana yellow jaguar had been seized by the tax office, so he was now riding around the town in a banana yellow smart car. His arrogance while driving remained as consistent as it had been previously.

To many of the locals, this produced a huge amount of amusement, but few people were so naive as to say anything to his face. Denzel, as everyone knew, could be a nasty piece of work, and although his grip on the town had weakened, he was working especially hard to tighten it again.

He already had a major role in the local branch of the Special Club, now he had ambitions to become one of the TWATS.

Denzel parked in a space at the end of the Millpool. Bill Dobson had a unit here next to Denzel's own.
Denzel knew that Bill used to take rubbish from some of the other businesses in the town, for a fee; and burn it in fires next to his unit. This was of course, Illegal.

Over time, Denzel had taken dozens of photographs of Bill doing this. He'd even managed to extract a couple of sworn statements from the business owners. It turned out they were happy to make use of Bills dubious service, but he wasn't a popular man, and in his case, they were happy to knife him in the back. After all, he would have done the same to them.

Bill had been the head man of the TWATS for two years, although everyone knew he was just a puppet. The other TWATS were the ones who really called the tune.
Denzel had leverage, Bill Dobson was connected, and so Denzel was about to make Bill an offer he couldn't possibly refuse.
Help Denzel or find himself being investigated by the local council.

Denzel knew that in order to join the TWATS, he first had to be approved by the existing TWATS.
It was a bit of a joke really. They were supposed to be a philanthropic organisation. Most of the town had long since recognised that they were nothing of the sort. Certainly not the core committee. Philanthropy couldn't have been further from their minds. Most of the TWATS were there to engage in back scratching, ego inflation and reinforcing their own fading sense of importance. Several of their organisation's activities were downright dishonest. Denzel desperately wanted to join.

Cowboy and Keith had asked Rob if he would take them out to meet a boat in the bay on the evening of Midsummers day.
Rob had been involved with boats for far too long to assume that any such meeting, especially with that pair, was anything other than criminal. He declined the offer. When Cowboy offered him £300 instead of the original £100, Rob was even more determined that whatever was going on, he wanted nothing to do with it.

Cowboy and Keith were sulking now, and they scowled at one another over pints of lager in one of the tow less salubrious pubs.
"We could use a couple of Jet skis?" Keith suggested.
"Kin you ride one?" Cowboy bounced back.
"Erm, well, No"
"And neither kin I. Next bright idea?" Cowboy was feeling particularly grumpy. He'd worked hard to sell the vodka they'd retrieved from Keveral Beach. Now he had almost three and a half thousand pounds, and he was desperate to buy more pills from the Dutchman before the Emmets began arriving in their droves.
He'd spoken to the Dutch supplier on the phone, and their rendezvous had been arranged. The problem was, it was looking as if they were going to have to use the kayak again. Cowboy was getting far too old for that nonsense.

He wondered if Cousin Denzel still had a boat. He hadn't spoken to Denzel since he'd come out of prison. Perhaps it was time to rectify that.

What they mustn't do was make any mention of the pills to him, he was bound to want a cut. That was going to be tricky.

It was also imperative that he didn't let Denzel go anywhere near his shed at Emmety Villa. There were still several hundred bottles in the big workshop. Most of the crates he'd 'borrowed' had gone to people who'd bought the vodka, but where he'd sold bottles in smaller quantities, he'd been left with a pile of empty crates.

Most of the vodka had been purchased by business owners, and so those crates would find their way back to Denzel's warehouse when the Looe spring water was delivered. The remaining crates had been fly tipped into the wood at the back of Emmety Villa. If Denzel saw those ones, Cowboy would have to provide an explanation.
Cowboy didn't like explanations, he had enough of that whenever his cousin Lowenna had him cornered.

His mind drifted as he took another swig. It was a shame he and Lowenna couldn't get along. Cousin she might be, but he'd fancied her for years. A lot of his acquaintances had been puzzled when he'd paired up with his current girlfriend. Most of them thought she was a rough old battle axe, and a gold digger. She was. The truth was though, she reminded Cowboy of his cousin. He wondered if he could get his girlfriend to dress up in a police uniform. He decided he'd offer her fifty quid and see if she'd go along with it.

Keith interrupted Cowboy's fantasy
"I heard Terry the Ferry is selling off some of his Doodlebugs" he offered.
This could be a solution, especially if the pills were going to become a regular business. "How much?" Cowboy answered.
"I don't know" replied Keith who then drained his glass

and tilted it towards his chum "You want another?"

"Yeah go on then, and then we can pop over the Petrie Dish, I think Terry still goes for coffees in there, and they sell beer"

"Cool" Keith stood up to go to the bar "This is much easier than antiques"

He couldn't have been more wrong.

Robbie the barman, was decanting one of the salvaged vodka bottles into a bottle with a label on it. He carefully replaced it on the optic. He had no conscience about this. Smuggling was an old and accepted tradition in Looe. Businesses paid far too much in tax and VAT. Robbie always said he wouldn't have minded, but the fact that some of it got spent on MP's fiddled expense claims irritated him.

If MP's and government officials could openly break the law and get away with it, Robbie saw nothing wrong with taking advantage of situations like the gift-of-the-sea-vodka. To Robbie's mind, he was helping to restore a little balance. He turned to face Keith. "Another couple?"

In the manager's office in the small supermarket, Jimmy hung up the phone. He was delighted. Not only had he secured his position as the new manager, but he had also been able to get his managers pay back dated to that truly horrible day at Easter.

He thought back on the events which had unfolded.
After Veryan had taken his keys, he and Rachael had clung to one another as they'd sobbed their hearts out for almost an hour. Eventually they'd managed to stop. Jimmy had showered and clambered into his work clothes. Rachael had administered a few of the eye drops she always kept in her bag.

When Jimmy arrived at the shop, it was chaos.
The morning crew had desperately rung around trying to find some keys and so the only saving grace was that all the staff except those who'd been partying the night before, had come to try to help.
Unfortunately, although they were doing their best, trying to restock the shop while fending off angry customers was proving to be a challenge.
The bread, milk and newspapers had been left outside. The seagulls had made the most of the opportunity and the little bread that was left was unsaleable. The cream and yoghurt had taken a serious hit too.
Inside the shop, there were half empty Rattler cans everywhere. No one knew where Dermot was.
By the time Jimmy rang the area manager to appraise him of the situation, the area manager already knew.
One of the local radio stations had broadcast that something unusual was happening in Looe at the small supermarket. The area manager arrived on the scene, along with around 400 curious members of the public who'd also

heard the story, just as Jimmy was hanging up.

With Marks help, Jimmy had explained what little they knew. The area manager, unable to handle such a situation himself, quickly put Jimmy in charge and left again. His degree in business studies might have opened the door to his elevated salary, but he had no idea whatsoever how to run a shop. He'd come back and see Jimmy after the Bank Holiday.

A little after 2pm, Dermot had been found. He was unconscious and smelt strongly of cider. Apparently, he'd constructed himself a nest from packs of toilet rolls, which he'd then screened off from the rest of the storeroom with a wall of boxes of crisps.
Later, Jimmy had called Dermot a taxi and asked Mark to see him safely home.

At the subsequent disciplinary hearing, Dermot had been demoted to General Assistant and told that if he wanted to continue his employment with the company, he'd have to go to the store in Helston. This was the Cornish version of being sent to Coventry.

Jimmy was now the manager, and he was making waves. The well-publicised court case Mark Wray had instigated against the owners of the Looe River View Hotel, had sent ripples of horror throughout the county. A great many of the abusive and exploitative practises some employers had allowed, were rapidly being corrected.
This included some of the practises within Jimmy's own firm. For the first time ever, Jimmy and his colleagues were being correctly paid for the hours they worked.
Mark Wray was a hero. Jimmy, who had the integrity to

stand up for his staff, was a hero too.

Rachael would be delighted. She was back at his flat seeing in the last of his boxes from the move. For the time being she would keep her own flat, and perhaps rent it to someone local when she moved into Emmety Villa full time. Decent housing was in short supply for local people and Jimmy and Rachael felt it a duty to try and help. Things were looking good.

Jimmy was especially pleased about the back pay. Terry the Ferry was selling off his Doodlebugs. Jimmy had wanted one for as long as he could remember.

The town was as busy as must be expected on a June Saturday in Looe.

Sargent Lowenna and WPC Veryan sat in the patrol car on the seafront discussing an old topic.

"I just can't work it out" Lowenna said in a frustrated tone. "I thought when we got that sleezy creep from Emmety Villa, that all this would stop."

"I know" Veryan answered her cousin "But we never did recover all the underwear, so I guess there were at least two panty perverts all along"

"Who on earth is it?" Lowenna asked again "And how come its happening in Looe *and* Polperro? You surely don't think it's another *two* of them, do you?"

Veryan took a deep breath as she pondered.

"Well, it's certainly a peculiar one. Who do we know that moves around at night in both places?"

"I don't know" Lowenna answered "But I bet the posties do, it's a bloody shame we can't ask them. What about the taxis?"

"Great idea" responded Veryan enthusiastically "I'll make some enquiries" by which she meant; she'd share some gossip with a few more of her cousins.

Lowenna looked at the people walking across the seafront. "Isn't that those two new couples who moved into Emmety?" She gestured towards the obelisk.

Donald and Sylvia and Norman and Marjorie were enjoying ice creams.

"Oh my god" gasped Veryan "It's history repeating itself. Oh-my-word, what do they think they look like?" She was horrified.

Sylvia and Marjorie were both wearing flesh-coloured leggings. Sylvias had tiger stripes and Marjorie's had leopard spots.

Lowenna laughed. "Well now, that looks like someone's been to Primark."

They continued to watch as Donald thrust an uneaten blue topped ice cream into one of the bins. It was immediately pulled out again by a herring gull.

"Is it the building?" Veryan asked "Does it do something to the people who stay there?"
"It must do love, our Alan and Eileen have been up the garden a lot lately, they've got outfits too."
"Yes, I heard" Veryan answered "What on earth are they doing?"

There weren't many secrets in a place as small as Looe.

"It's witchcraft by the looks of it" Lowenna continued, "There's no need to worry though, they're good people. I'd give you a lot more for Alan and Eileen than I would some of this lot. Oh look, guess who?"

A distinctive looking banana yellow Smart car pulled up outside Denzel's Plaice, the fish and chip shop. Denzel spotted the police car just in time and turned the engine back on. He'd have to park legally somewhere today. Lowenna and Veryan lip read as Denzel swore, and then waved at him as he drove past. As Denzel turned the corner by the RNLI building, the two police officers had a good laugh.
"What's he up to now?" Veryan wondered out loud.
"I have it on good authority that he's trying to join the TWATS" Lowenna answered.
I thought he already was one?"

The laughter continued for quite some time.

Bill Dobson was explaining what had happened at his meeting with Denzel Sprygelly. It wasn't an official meeting of the Town Welcome And Tourist Support, so the four core members had gathered at Alan Badcock's house.
The other two conspirators were Ryan Smugly and John Dory.

Denzel it transpired, had been watching the activities of the TWATS for some time now, and he'd used his extensive list of contacts to extract a great deal more valuable information about their activities.
For instance, some of the contracts they'd handed their tenants, contained clauses which were unlawful. The provisions they made for their staff and their contracts had dubious omissions too.

Denzel had somehow managed to obtain the organisations financial records. Considering the organisation was supposed to act in the best interests of the town, including their tenants, it was quite clear the TWATS were failing spectacularly in fulfilling their obligations.

Despite this, at Christmas every year, they would host a lavish, all expenses paid dinner in one of the more expensive restaurants, in order to congratulate themselves; all at the expense of the organisation.

The four worked together regularly. Denzel had intimated terms such as 'Conspiracy to screw over all the tenants' and 'dishonest collusion while making decisions without consulting the whole of the committee'

Denzel had also managed to dig up personal dirt on all of them. He'd given Dobson four envelopes which the

TWATS took to different corners of the room to open privately.

Badcock was a well-known bully. He'd been beaten publicly as a result of it, one New Year's Eve when he'd picked on the wrong person. He was known to be cocky in the town and was probably a lot more intensely disliked than he realised. Denzel had somehow managed to find out that alongside his regular business, Badcock also printed and circulated a magazine for swingers. There was a copy of one edition in his envelope.
In a small town like Looe, that was one little gem Badcock most definitely couldn't afford to become known.

Dobson had his illegal refuse removal business going, and there were the photos he'd already seen. He had also been involved in several shady business deals, including a few with Denzel himself. There were four pages of notes about this. He had to confess this now to the other TWATS. Denzel had even suggested that Dobson had used his TWATS connections, to influence and further his own business aims in the town. This was clearly a conflict of interests and should never have been allowed.
Unfortunately for Dobson, Denzel had been correct.

Denzel hadn't been able to find out much about John Dory's business interests, or Smugly, but what he did have was a pile of incriminating photographs.

Dory was clearly taking money regularly from Charity Sally. He also frequently sent people to her. There were also photos of another local celebrity 'Mandy the maneater' as she was known. Dory took money from her too, and sometimes gave Mandy lifts to various hotels around the town. Dory was in short, a pimp. Dory's envelope had photos, receipts and a memory card that Denzel had somehow obtained which held recordings of telephone calls

Lastly came Smugly. There was no doubt he was the man Lowenna and Veryan were looking for. There were photographs of him dressed in a skin-tight cat-suit type affair, removing lady's underwear from at least half a dozen different washing lines in an assortment of locations. Smugly was livid. The photographer had clearly captured his face.

How the hell had Denzel accumulated all this? Clearly Mr Sprygelly had been busy for a long time before his little holiday.

Two hours of shouting ensued.

Terry the Ferry pushed his plate away and almost instantly felt a gripe in his bowels. "I'll be right back" he told Jimmy and Rachael "It's the old tum. I've had the runs for weeks, no bloomin idea what's causing it" with which, he moved hurriedly towards the door of the toilet at the rear of the café.

Rachael and Jimmy exchanged knowing looks. The Petrie Dish was getting an appalling reputation. Most of the customers only went in once, and so they never realised the source of their troubles. A few locals though, intending to help support a new business, had adopted this as their new regular. Mostly they were there for the entertainment. Ronald tended to bluster his way through things. He liked to think he was a lot cleverer than most of his customers, and he would share the benefit of his knowledge on many subjects whenever there was a lull, which was frequent. Terry and a few of the fishermen who'd begun to come in for the show, found it all hilarious.

It hadn't taken long before the stomach upsets and incidents of chronic diarrhoea had begun.
Sales of what the staff referred to as anti-squit-pills, had gone up five-fold in the little supermarket.
Jimmy and Rachael had gone for the safe option, two bottles of sparkling Looe water. Rachael wiped the tops again with a steri-wipe.
"Are you sure this is what you really want?" She asked Jimmy again.
Jimmy nodded and smiled.

Unknown to Rachael, Jimmy had been taking an on-line assertiveness training workshop for several weeks now. While Rachael was at work presenting the weather forecast on telly, Jimmy had been working his way towards a new certificate.

Rachael had no idea that it was this which had changed the dynamic in their bedroom, and several other locations, including the back of the bacon counter.

Rachael was liking the new Jimmy.

Jimmy was taking his newfound confidence and was applying it to all sorts of situations. It was helping hugely at work. He wasn't embarrassed when he bought condoms anymore, and he was even learning to stand up to some of the idiots who attempted to harass the staff in his shop. This week's challenge was going to be, to have a word with that idiot Nigel who kept parking in Jimmy's parking space. Jimmy didn't own a car, but that wasn't the point.

Rachael smiled at her beloved. A Doodlebug would be lovely, even if it did mean they wouldn't be having an en-suite in Jimmy's new flat after all.

That had been an interesting discussion. Jimmy had pointed out rightly that the existing bathroom worked perfectly well, and anyway, wouldn't having an en-suite be a bit like having a poo in the corner of the bedroom?

Rachael had to concede that yes, she'd rather their morning extrusions occurred in a location somewhere away from the place they enjoyed their passions.

Ronald came to clear away Terry's plate and proceeded to wipe the table with a filthy cloth.

"Ere, in't you that girl wot does the wevver on the telly?"
Rachael, always pleased to be recognised, smiled broadly.
"That's right, I'm Rachael, Rachael De Sprygelly"
"Well then" Ronald continued in his grating accent "If you're that good at the wevver, can you predict the lottery?" He laughed at his own joke and picked up the

trayful of breakfast things.

Fortunately, at that point Terry emerged from the lavatory. "Shall we go and have a look at the boats?" He offered brightly.

Jimmy and Rachael hurriedly climbed to their feet.

Without another word they headed towards the door. Terry followed.

Once the door had closed behind them, Jimmy asked Terry "Who is that idiot?"

"Oh that's the famous Ronald" Terry answered.

"Well, I can't see that business lasting long" Rachael joined in.

"I don't think he plans to" Terry continued "He's got a room over the estate agents, says he's going to offer Reiki and counselling"

"Really?" Rachael's eyes widened and then she laughed. She'd noticed a board advertising someone who could apparently sort out your whole life for just £75 an hour. Unfortunately, whoever had written the board had used the wrong spelling and put councelling. He'd spelt Reiki incorrectly too. The word on the board had been spelt Riekie. Rachael wasn't convinced Ronald knew his subjects very well.

They laughed as Jimmy cracked the old joke. Most villages only had one idiot.

Looe is a place where the activity peaks and troughs and the Mill pool car park is a perfect barometer of just how busy the town is.

In winter, the town seems to be asleep. Many of the businesses are closed. Day trippers and out of season holiday makers often don't understand why.
In a town where so much of the residential accommodation has become second homes and holiday lets, it's not easy keeping a business going when there's no one there to use it.

The local authority kept granting permission for even more new houses to be built on the green fringes, while the life slowly bled out of the heart of the town.
The back streets, which were in reality, the front streets; were so devoid of life in winter, they could have been used for a post apocalypse television drama. Where local people used to squabble with their neighbours over whose cat had crapped in whose flower tub, the streets now echoed only to the cooing of hungry pigeons.
Where there were once news agents and butchers, haberdashery shops and greengrocers, now there were pasty shops and corporate retailers masquerading as charity shops.
In winter, the charity shops only stayed open because they were staffed by volunteers. The pasty shops were closed.

Locals greeted one another in the town and the few who didn't depend on tourism or who must drive through the main street by necessity, were happy.

In January and February, easterly gales lashed the town with a ferocity the summer visitors could never imagine.

Water pushed up through the drainage grates and the tarmac roads became waterways. It would be quite beautiful if it weren't so damaging.
The good people took the positives wherever they could, as at least it washed away the dog eggs.

The first sign that life was returning, was a brief flurry in Mid-February. "You've been a Dick all year, now treat her to a nice meal" read the advertising for valentines' banquets. And "Nothing says I love you more than a ludicrously priced bouquet" at the petrol station.
Valentines fell at the same time as half term, although how the two were compatible is anyone's guess. Perhaps it was a subtle type of organised contraception?

There was a brief flurry as visitors trickled into the town in a desperate bid to snatch a few moments away from their lives beyond the Tamar Bridge. If they had been charged to come into the county, the council tax bills could have been halved. Instead, they were charged to leave, so Plymouth city council could afford all the policing it needed.

From then on there was a different flurry of activity as walls and windows were repainted, carpets and equipment were replaced in holiday lets; and a few brave hopefuls began to arrive. The ambitious ones left the comfort of their holiday cottages and set out for bracing walks along the cliff paths. Others found a welcoming fire in a pub and would spend the week in an alcohol induced daze.

By April, there was another flurry. This time the holiday camps were beginning to open, albeit with reduced entertainments. Chocolate Sunday passed, the schools re-opened, and the business owners ticked along serving the newly-weds and nearly-dead until June, when things really began to lift off.

Each weekend the car parks became a little fuller, the streets busier, and Denzel and his fellows plotted more and more ingenious ways to relieve tourists of their hard-earned cash.

There were festivals and carnivals, music days and water events. The sun shone lighting up the whole valley. Tills rattled with pound coins and the seagulls feasted on fast food plucked skilfully from the paws of the naïve and inexperienced.

By August, the place was as full as it could get. Lobster coloured acres of flesh oozed across the beach. Pasties and Ice creams were consumed by the thousand. People laughed and smiled, employees became exhausted and emotionally frazzled, and Denzel and his ilk cruised their businesses repeating the mantra "Just keep smiling and taking the money."
In the small supermarket, as in many of the bars and cafes, the staff tolerated varying degrees of rudeness, impatience and abuse.

The day the schools went back, it was as if someone had flicked a switch. The whole town breathed a huge sigh of relief, the tension abated, and the pace of life returned to something a lot less frantic.

Now was when the newly-weds and nearly-dead returned. Coaches full of couples like Sylvia and Donald and their friends, Norman and Marjorie, decanted their occupants who then went eagerly questing cream teas and commemorative tea towels and teaspoons.

Gradually the town wound down again. The last flurry was the October half term. Sometimes the holidaying families saw a few sunny days. Sometimes they spent the entire time avoiding the storms, newly arrived from the Atlantic and dragging the tail ends of hurricanes with them.
By November, only the people who live here remained.

For a week at Christmas the pubs were packed and again, people desperate to escape their lives packed into holiday cottages and seafront apartments. The staff in the small supermarket swiftly exchanged displays of mince pies for displays of easter eggs, and then the cycle began again.

For the people living in the town, May and June were probably the best months there were. The weather was pleasant, the gardens and verges were full of flowers. The businesses which had survived another tough winter had re-opened, and it was possible to walk from one end of the town to the other without running the gauntlet of thousands of visitors and their erratic behaviour.

At Emmety Villa, June was going to be a particularly busy month.

Cowboy had been given the job of maintaining Emmety Villa. There was a lot to do. The previous owner of the freehold had collected all the ground rents, but then failed to maintain the building.

Cowboy had been given the job the year before when no one else had been available. All the builders with a good reputation were always booked up for months in advance.

There had been so many changes of occupants in the last few years that Alan and Eileen hadn't known who had bought the freehold until today.

It was Denzel.

Alan could have wept. Eileen was a little more optimistic, she hadn't just been studying witchcraft since last summer, she was also studying law as a mature student. Eileen was getting quite familiar with the laws around properties.

She reassured Alan. "It's fine love, we'll do some magic and all we have to do is use the law"

"But you know what he's like, he'll try and throw his weight around like he usually does"

Eileen had looked up a section of the Landlord and Tenant Act. "He won't get very far. If he thinks he can come up here playing lord of the manor and shooting his mouth off, he's going to get a shock. Have a look at this". She indicated section 11 of the act. "If he tries messing anyone up here about, I'll get our Lowenna to arrest him!" Eileen finished triumphantly.

Denzel might well own the freehold, but that meant far more responsibilities than privileges, and Eileen knew the law far better than Denzel.

The work had been deemed essential by the inspector from the local council, and so no matter who owned the freehold, it was going ahead.

Denzel would be the one who received the bill now, and there was nothing he could do about it.
"I wonder who duped him into buying it?" Eileen laughed.

Downstairs, Marjorie and Sylvia were sharing coffee while gazing out at the beautiful view. The woods had turned green again at last and the river sparkled in the strong sunlight. Norman and Donald had gone out for a stroll. The girls knew this meant they'd gone to the pub.
"What are they up to this time then?" Marjorie asked.
Sylvia had already seen the catalogues and on-line sales sites Donald that had been studying.
"I'm pretty certain they plan to buy a poly tunnel. Donald has been wonderfully successful with his Cannabis plants the last few years. I don't know what I'd do without it" she added "My arthritis has virtually disappeared"
"Oh of course" Marjorie acknowledged. "No wonder Norman was looking at the packets of seeds he had saved. He's quite good at it too you know." She smiled at Sylvia before continuing. "Changing the subject, how are things in, you know, other departments."
Marjorie smiled back. The two, like their husbands, had become firm friends over the last few months, and they were far to worldly to have secrets or be embarrassed by anything.
"I'd really like to get a few more of those blue pills if we can get them. Norman is willing, but without them, he's a bit like Jesus"
Sylvia pulled a puzzled face. Marjorie continued.
"Like Jesus at Easter, after three days, he rises again"
Sylvia laughed. "I used to call Donald's todger 'Mr Pinkwhistle', these days he's more like Lazarus"
Eileen and Alan could hear the laughter upstairs.

At a table, outside the pub on the corner, Donald passed the remains of a small spliff to Norman. They were still discussing their new poly tunnel. Every time they referred to it as their 'joint venture' they'd start to laugh again like a pair of naughty schoolboys.

Norman took a long pull and then quickly flicked the roach into the ashtray as it began to burn his fingers.

"Hmmm, nice gear that, where did you say you got it again?"

Donald had a mouthful of cider before answering "It was one of the blokes down on the seafront by the shelter. He said he used to be the Mayor here. Now he sells a bit of weed every now and then, just to finance his own use he said"

Norman thought about this for a few moments.

"Could he be a potential customer then? If we fill a twenty metre one, we're going to have loads more than we can use ourselves"

Donald had another mouthful of cider and paused for thought before answering "Yes, I suppose so. I'm not keen on growing masses, but we'd be in just as much trouble for a hundred plants as if we only had ten, so we might as well fill our boots"

"Agreed" Norman answered and lifted his glass "Here's to our joint venture"

The pair of old codgers collapsed in hysterics.

As Donald and Norman continued to make plans, Cowboy clambered down from the scaffolding which wrapped around the rear of Emmety Villa. He'd decided to make the job last as long as possible, which had been one of his tactics for decades anyway. The longer the work took, the longer it would be before he had to move out of the storage sheds that were a part of the property. Originally, they'd existed as a coach house and stables for the grand house, long before it's conversion into apartments.

Cowboy knew that if his cousins, Lowenna and Veryan, ever suspected him of anything, they would have no reticence at all in searching his house. Consequently, he was grateful to be able to come and go freely at Emmety, and still maintain a degree of deniability.
Right now, it was time for a few quick vodkas and a snooze. He'd been working for almost an hour and a half now anyway, so that was his day finished. He'd have a nap in the shed before going round to his girlfriend's B&B.
He was looking forward to this evening. His girlfriend had accepted his offer to dress as a female police sergeant. It had cost him a hundred quid, not the fifty he'd intended, but he reckoned it would be worth it.

Sylvia and Marjorie emerged from the front doors. They'd decided to join their husbands in the pub.
Cowboy was deeply impressed with their leggings. Animal print was in this year. Sylvia had zebra stripes, and Marjorie was wearing the leopard spot pair again. They were lucky blokes those two fellas Cowboy thought to himself.

Denzel sat in the large chair behind the desk in the head TWATS office, being briefed on what was about to happen by Bill Dobson.

Dobson had worked his way down the list of tasks the committee hoped to accomplish and came to the final note. "…..and from Monday, Employment Compliance Officer Mark Wray will be here"

Denzel blanched. He had history with Mark Wray, and during Denzel's little Holiday, Mark had successfully turned over several stones Denzel would much rather had been left unturned. He climbed to his feet.

"You lot can deal with him" he announced to the rather cowered Dobson "I shall take up my new position when he's gone." With that, he picked up his hat, and marched promptly out of the office. To reinforce his displeasure, Dobson heard Denzel slam the main door on his way out of the building"

Dobson was confused. After all the shouting, it had been reluctantly agreed to allow Denzel to join the gang of four, just as long as certain things were kept from him.
The existing cohorts had far too much at stake to allow Denzel to humiliate them. Better to get him involved, and then break him from the inside they'd reasoned.

Now Denzel had walked out, and he wouldn't be back for some time if Mark Wray were as thorough as he usually was. Thank god Mark Wray's remit only covered looking at the way the TWATS treated their staff and not a full financial audit.

They'd had extra time since the Looe River View court case, and so most things were above board now, but they hadn't been for an exceedingly long time before that.

The committee had incurred some big expenses getting Robin Hood Roy to produce a new false set of payroll accounts. The handful of employees had needed new contracts of employment too.

The idea had been to allow Denzel to occupy the chairman's seat and then let him take all the flack when the end of year accounts were published. These would be the special accounts, which again, had been especially prepared by accountant, Robin Hood Roy.

Dobson did what he always did when there was a decision to be made, he rang Smugly.

Smugly snapped down the phone at Dobson that "now is not a good time" and quickly hung up. He turned his attention back to his friend who was sipping a Gin and tonic on Smugly's patio. "Sorry about that, you were telling me how many parcels you can deliver to me?" he said to the Dutchman.

As the sun set on the town for another day, Denzel Sprygelly counted twenty-pound notes at his desk in his office at home. He missed his office in the town, but things had changed a lot and it was an overhead he'd had to cut back on. He'd sub-let the three room flat over the chip shop to one of his nephews. He was earning more in rent than he'd been paying for it in the first place. His lease said he wasn't allowed to sub-let, but no-one was checking so he did it anyway. If there wasn't an inspection by the fire service, no one would know he was breaking yet another law.

In Denzel's mind, he could do whatever he wanted. He'd gone to prison once, but he'd soon been let out again, and the investigations into his affairs hadn't begun to scratch the surface of his dishonest dealings.

Denzel was feeling happy, not to mention smug.

In Emmety Villa, Donald and Sylvia were enjoying dinner with Norman and Marjorie. They'd agreed to a nine O'clock finish. They were all mature enough to admit that the nights of staying up until daybreak were a long way behind them. Nine thirty was a late night these days, and excited as they were with their new homes and the glorious view over the river, they liked to be tucked up with their hot water bottles by nine thirty at the latest.

Jimmy was still at work. The shop closed at 10pm. He would have to cash up and then Rachael, who wouldn't get home from the television studio herself until 10pm; would be waiting to tell him all about her day.

Jimmy was eager to tell her all about his progress with the Doodlebug, but that would probably have to wait until after he'd considered her lustful desires.

Lowenna and Veryan were both on late turn. Their mission was to try and catch the Looe and Polperro Knicker nicker. They'd parked the police car at the top of the town and walked to a place they could observe the goings on from the top of the hill at the area of meadows known as the Wooldown. Lowenna had drawn two pairs of night vision binoculars from supplies. They were so engrossed in scanning the town, that they were oblivious to the taxi leaving Ryan Smugly's house, not far from their current vantage point.

The Dutchman had said goodnight to Smugly and climbed into the back seat. The taxi had left the town quietly, but now, less than a mile from Smugly's house, it had pulled over in a layby.

"Do you want to drive boss?" The driver turned to the back seat.
"I've had a drink Chris, so best not eh?" The Dutchman replied, but he no longer affected a Dutch accent. In fact, he sounded rather like a Plymothian. "I'll get in the front though, if you don't mind." It was a statement, not a request.

The back door opened, legs swayed, and DI Bernard Flood of Plymouth CID clambered into the front seat of the car.
"How was it boss?" Chris, the driver enquired.
"Pretty good actually Chris. I think our little trawl is going to catch quite a few of the bottom feeders this time" Bernard smiled and continued "It's just like my nephew said. On the face of it, they're all respectable and law abiding. When you dig a bit deeper though, some of this lot are so rotten and corrupt, they make Lucifer himself look like one of the good guys"

Chris put the car in gear and pulled back out onto the road.
"Sir, I hope you don't mind me saying, but I'm a bit uncomfortable about when we used those ecstasy tablets as bait"
Bernard laughed. "It's okay lad, you can rest easy, they weren't ecstasy tablets"
Chris butted in before his superior could continue.
"But the surveillance said the people who'd had them were going for it like it was a Beatles love-in?"
The power of suggestion Chris" Bernard reassured him. "There wasn't anything unlawful in the tablets we had the boat drop off as bait"
"But they danced and did all sorts of stuff" the uncertainty in Chris's voice was plain. He'd seen the close surveillance footage, even for the three Mexicans dancing on the beach.
"Mostly alcohol and a little suggestion" Bernard reassured him and then laughed "Mind you, I might be tempted to try one myself"
Chris was horrified, he braked abruptly.
"Sir!"
Bernard carried on laughing.
"Get us home Chris and stop fretting. The blue ones were ginseng, nothing illegal in that, and the white ones…" he threw his head back as he let out an almighty barrage of laughter "They were dogs worm tablets"
"Really?" Chris let the new information sink in.
"Yes. Really. Need to know lad" Bernard tapped his nose. "This is a special op, you know we can't be transparent at this stage, even to our own people. Need to know."
Bernard tapped his nose again to emphasise the point.
"Now come on then young Christopher, lets go home"

In the Looe River View hotel, Paul Sprygelly wiped down the bar as the last of the customers thanked him and headed back to their rooms. The Chef called him quietly from the door of the kitchen. "Loads left tonight, do you want any?"

Paul looked at the platter the chef was holding. It had sausages on sticks, cheese footballs and vol au vents.

He decided to pass and shook his head. The last time he'd eaten a vol au vent, he'd felt quite strange for three days afterwards. He'd been feeling emotionally fragile, and he'd needed multiple visits to the lavatory. On the bright side though, his bum had stopped itching for the first time since he'd been in the hotel business, and for the first time in his life, he'd begun to put weight on.

In his apartment in Emmety Villa, Alan was wearing the wizard outfit again. He'd opened the door to the postman a few minutes previously. The postman had handed Alan his packet without a second glance. Alan supposed that if you did that sort of job, you got to see people wearing all sorts of things. It was true, but sometimes the poor posties got to see things they'd rather they hadn't. The postie had continued with his round, grateful that he didn't have to deliver to Maurice at number one anymore. Maurice used to come to the door naked. He used to peer around the partially opened door to receive his mail. Unfortunately, while this process took place, Maurice's tackle would be pressed up against the inside of the door. The door was made of glass.
By comparison, Alan in his wizard outfit was positively pedestrian. He shut the main door behind him and hopped over the low fence that separated Emmety Villa from Adrian next door. There was no sign of either Adi or Ed the donkey, they must have gone for a walk on the beach.

There was another knock on the door, Alan thought it must be the postman returning, perhaps he'd forgotten something?
What Alan hadn't anticipated was that it was Donald and Norman who would be standing on his doorstep.
There was an uncomfortable silence as the pair took in Alan's star covered robes and pointy shoes. Alan for his part was unabashed, he gestured towards his kitchen inviting them in. "Do come in, please, have a seat. How can I help you gentlemen?"

Donald and Norman supressed their sniggers and took a seat each. Alan followed suit and listened attentively. Norman began. "We were wondering how you'd feel about us putting up a poly tunnel."

Alan had been thinking about something similar himself. His time in the garden centre, and the success of Adi next door in his, made the proposal something well worth considering.

"Interesting" Alan answered thoughtfully. It would have to go right at the top, up by the woods. It's south facing so it would get plenty of sunlight up there. How big were you thinking, and what are you thinking of growing?"

"We thought twenty metres" Donald answered.

"Cannabis" Norman added.

"Oh!" Alan had been expecting them to say tomatoes.

There was another uncomfortable silence until Donald added, "It's purely medicinal, Sylvias hips you know, arthritis"

"Oh I see" Alan slowly nodded before continuing, "Well, you'd have to ask upstairs and Kirsten from number three when she comes back" He gestured a thumb in the general direction of the other occupant of Emmety Villas front door. "but I don't see why not" he said reflectively "From what I remember from the garden centre, quite a few of my old customers used to do the same thing"

Alan knew just how many quite a few was. He'd regularly been asked to supply a certain type of plant food and his customers had confided in him what they'd been cultivating, purely for medicinal purposes of course.

There was a thud from upstairs as Rachael busied herself in her kitchen.

"You'll probably get a green light from Jimmy and Rachael"

This time Alan gestured towards the ceiling. "I think they're too involved in their passions to be involving themselves in the garden at the moment"

"Oh that's what that noise is" replied Norman looking thoughtful. "Marjorie and I thought it was next doors donkey"

Just then Eileen came through to the kitchen and immediately picked up on the conversation.

"No, it's definitely not Ed. Rachael certainly knows how to let herself go" and she winked at Alan.

"Golly!" said Norman and Donald in unison.

Alan gave an involuntary shudder as he recalled the beastly noises which had been coming from upstairs since Jimmy and Rachael had taken up residence. He made a mental note that he really must get some more soundproofing on the ceilings.

"I couldn't bloody believe it!" Lowenna was explaining to Veryan how another two pairs of her well scaffolded knickers had vanished from her washing line. "That's the third bloody time since Easter"

They were in the patrol car again and Lowenna had driven up to the road where she lived to explain what had happened yet again.

Veryan nodded sympathetically to her Sargent. They'd been trying to find the knicker nicker for over a year now. Whoever it was had been busy, and they still had nothing to go on.

Lowenna was especially annoyed as she'd been particularly vigilant lately. She wasn't supposed to be working until this evening but there were things that needed to be sorted out.

They'd thought it would end when Maurice had been locked up, but it hadn't, if anything, it was worse.

Lowenna, frustrated and angry continued. "The only thing I know for certain is that for once, Cousin Denzel isn't the guilty one."

Veryan was intrigued. "Do we know that for certain?"

Lowenna huffed. "It didn't stop when he was doing his time did it? We both know what a devious, dishonest scheming toe-rag he is, but I don't think we can attribute this to him, just this once"

Veryan nodded again.

"Whoever it is can certainly cover a lot of ground. There's only one road in the whole town now where there hasn't been an incident."

This peeked Lowenna's interest. "Hmm, and where might that be?"

"Up the top of lung-buster Hill" Veryan answered giving the road in question it's local name. "Up by where that

TWAT Smugly lives."
"I think we need to give that some thought then."
Lowenna finished and changed the subject.
"We'd better go and sort out this fun-run business."
She turned the key in the ignition, and they set off to visit the chairman of the local Lions group.

The Looe Holiday camp and Hotel Mascot race was the next big event in the busy calendar. There might be as many as 50 entrants this year. Lowenna and Veryan both knew it would be a combination of Fun-run, a huge public turn out, a day when a lot of alcohol was consumed, and more than likely, an occasional squabble.
Just another normal working day then.

Lowenna was always happy to help out when the Lions hosted events. Unlike some of the other clubs in the town, the members weren't always glory seeking or looking for a photo opportunity. It had been said of one of the councillors for instance, that he'd turn up for the opening of a bag of crisps if he thought there was a photo opportunity in it for him. The councillor in question was hoping to graduate to full MP one day, at which point he'd be able to treat herself to a whole new wardrobe, on expenses of course.

The Mascot fun run would follow the same route as the Easter parade, and the carnival, and the three-legged charity pub crawl, and the December Santa fun run. In fact, all the parades followed the same route. Lowenna thought it would be nice if for once, things were arranged differently. Perhaps the runners could go down to the seafront having started at the eastern end of the bridge. They could loop back along the quay, and then go over to the west side.

She said as much to Veryan who thought about it for a few minutes and then said, "It would probably cause a riot, most of this lot just aren't ready for change."

It was true, and that was exactly why the same people, people like Denzel Sprygelly and Bill Dobson and Ryan Smugly, always had such a strong grip on the town. Change *was* possible, but apathy generally won the day.

Lowenna shrugged her shoulders. "Yes love, you're right of course. I suppose in some ways it's reassuring to have the same routines, but it doesn't leave much room for anything new or original does it?"
Veryan thought for a minute again before replying. "No, I guess it doesn't, but then new and different isn't always better either. Remember that time that Cockney tried to get everyone to paint their houses Irish style?"
Lowenna did indeed remember. In Kinsale and Cork and Bantry, the mixture of yellow and green and blue house fronts made a prominent and colourful statement.
In Looe, it had been a surrealist nightmare. The only masonry paint available at Trago at the time had been either orange or purple. The back streets had looked like a 1970's bathroom.
Fortunately, people soon realised the enormity of their mistakes and the houses had returned to less glaring colours.

Lowenna had good reason to re-route the runners. It would mean opening the gates along the quay and letting traffic through an area which was now restricted. Since the fish market had closed, there was no valid argument not to let delivery vehicles use that access again, and it would benefit the town.

Of course, a handful of people would object. Like a great many towns, it was all quite territorial.
There was also something about Lowenna's sense of humour in her idea. Perhaps the former fish market should be where the finish line was? After all, it had been the place so many mackerel and crabs had been landed.

An hour later, a victorious Lowenna had managed to persuade the former fisherman, now a prominent Lion, to end the run at the fish market building.
Apart from the short section on the seafront, most of the route would be covered by CCTV. If previous years were anything to go by, this might be a particularly good thing. The race was scheduled for the first Sunday in August, around seven weeks away. This wasn't an ideal time to have to run a course of almost a mile and a half in a heavy costume, but it had become a tradition now, and the visitors loved it, especially when it went awry, as it inevitably did.

It was delivery day at Emmety Villa. Donald and Norman had prepared the ground and now the construction phase was due to begin. Jimmy was having a rare Saturday off and so he was outside waiting to help his new neighbours. Alan was there too. He'd put his garden centre overalls on and was keen to get started. Alan was a veteran of several Poly tunnel erections and he knew that although it looked simple, it rarely was. Adi had left Ed tethered to a post on a long rope in his own garden and had climbed over the short fence to offer his assistance too. It would be a proper community effort.

Rachael had gone to join Marjorie and Sylvia on the patio. Eileen would join them shortly. The plan had been to set a date for one of Marjorie's sex toys parties. The men would be excluded of course. Rachael marvelled at Marjorie's confidence and energy. She hoped she would have that much get-up-and-go when she was almost seventy-five like Marjorie did now. When it came to Rachael and exercise, her get-up-and-go had got-up-and-gone when she was twenty, although it seemed to come back whenever she and Jimmy had a private moment. Eileen arrived with a bottle of gin and a big bottle of tonic. "Thought we might get an early one in while they play their man games." She winked at the three seated ladies.

The text message had told the men that their tunnel would arrive between 10.30 and 11am. At 10.31 a DPD van pulled up at the bottom of the steps and the five men went down to assist the greatly relieved driver. The Poly tunnel had come packed into four large packets. Alan, Donald and Norman took one each, while Adi and Jimmy struggled with the tube containing the heavy polythene cover.

Jimmy and Adi had almost made it to the top of the first flight of steps when Rachael shouted "Adi, I think your mates going for a walk"

Adi looked up in dismay just in time to see Ed disappearing into the wood at the top of the garden. Clearly the rope hadn't been properly secured. "Oh Hell!" Adi exclaimed, "Sorry mate, I'd better get him before he takes off" he looked quickly at Jimmy and dropped his end of the package. "No worries mate, do you want a hand?" Jimmy offered by way of reply. Adi, grateful for any help he could get quickly answered "Yes please, but when we get close, just don't run at him, he'll get scared."

"No problem" answered the amiable supermarket manager now dropping his end too. The two set off at a brisk pace up the slope towards the rapidly disappearing donkey.

By the time they got to the top of the garden, Ed was nowhere to be seen.

Adi bent forward with his hands on his knees, he was panting after the sprint up the steep slope.

"Oh god" he groaned before explaining to an equally breathless Jimmy. "Last time he got out; he went back to his old stable at Hilltop farm."

Jimmy had recovered just enough to speak. "That's not so bad then, at least we know where to look."

"That's not the big issue." Adi continued between gasps. Jimmy didn't understand and Adi had to explain in a bit more detail. "He knows how to open gates."

Jimmy still didn't understand why this was a problem and his face clearly showed this.

Adi continued. "He's friends with the alpacas. The last time he was up there, he opened the gate to their field."

Jimmy knew the place well. At one time it had been called

Pigs R Us. Anything pig related, from bacon to piggy banks could be bought here. Then Peppa Pig had come along and the whole thing had been ruined.

These days there were alpacas. First there were two, then six, and the last time Jimmy had walked along the coast path that way, he'd counted at least twenty of the teddy bear faced animals. If Ed opened the gate now, there would be chaos.

"We'd better get moving" Jimmy looked back at Adi and fished in his pocket for his phone. "I'd better ring the old bill too and let the control room know." Adi nodded. "Good idea. Perhaps they can get hold of him. It would be terrible if he got hurt." And then in a quieter voice added. "I love that donkey, he's a real character."

Jimmy made the call and the two set off in pursuit of Ed. The older gentlemen would have to manage without them for a while.

While Jimmy and Adi went looking for Ed, Cowboy and Uncle Keith were inspecting their latest acquisition. Cowboy had reluctantly handed Two thousand pounds to Terry the Ferry and he was now the owner of what had been referred to in the town, as a Doodlebug.

The Doodlebugs, so called because of the put putting of their engines, were beautiful. They'd been lovingly maintained. The Doodlebugs were small, clinker-built boats with diesel engines, configured and modified so that almost anyone could use one. Most of Looe's fleet had been hired out to visitors on an hour-by-hour basis. They were a part of the towns heritage and people loved them. It was a tragic day when health and safety legislation madness, firmly put an end to their use.

They were still allowed to be used privately though, and Cowboy felt it was a worthwhile investment. In normal circumstances he'd have 'borrowed' one, but the little boy in him had been desperate to own one for years anyway. Now he had an excuse. His girlfriend would be livid if she'd known how much money he'd just spent. He was learning he had to keep his financial affairs to himself rapidly though, and her increasing interest in his bank account was starting to ring alarm bells.

The little boat was currently moored up next to the boatyard. A few steps down a ladder and the pair were in.
"Shall we go for a ride then?" Keith suggested.
"I reckon we ought to." Cowboy replied, and he sat by the wheel and pushed the primer followed by the start button. The engine fired first time.
Like the children they were, Cowboy and Uncle Keith let loose a volley of excited squeals that up on the hillside,

even the current occupants of the garden of Emmety Villa could hear.

"Cast away" cried Keith as he undid the wrong end of the mooring rope and tossed it back towards the post set into the quayside. In a few short moments, they were passing under the bridge which linked East and West Looe and heading out to sea.
"Let's go to Polperro and have a beer." Cowboy suggested.
"Great idea" Keith called back over the noise of the Lister engine.

The pair made a big show of shouting to everyone they knew on either side of the river as they worked their way towards the end of the banjo pier. They passed the White Rock, and for once, made a sensible decision not to try the shallow channel between Hannafore and the island. They headed due south to go around St Georges Island by the long route.

They were almost at the reef marker when the engine ran out of fuel and abruptly died.
"Oh dammitt!" Cowboy would have stamped his foot if he hadn't been seated.
"What do we do now?" asked Keith. There were rollicks in the central locker in the little boat, but they'd neglected to load the oars on board in their haste to show off.
It was cold on the water; it always is when the wind blows. Neither was properly dressed.

Overhead, the seagulls circled them with mocking cries. Cowboy climbed achily to his feet and began waving at the shore. A little girl on the end of the Banjo waved back. The boat began to drift towards the island, but then a

gentle westerly wind blew then back again.
Things continued much the same way for the next four hours.

Terry the Ferry was oblivious to what was going on just offshore. He'd sold two of his boats today. It saddened him greatly to see the end of the tradition. He'd looked after all his boats; they'd been maintained to a far higher standard than practically any of the pleasure boats that now filled the moorings all the way up the river.

He sat at his usual table in the Petrie Dish and patiently waited for Ronald to bring him the egg and chips he'd ordered. He could feel the reassuring wad of notes in his jeans pocket. He wondered what Cowboy and Uncle Keith were up to, no good he expected. Where those two went, there was bound to be something nefarious occurring.

The other boat had been purchased by Ryan Smugly. Smugly had obviously given the matter a lot more thought and had come prepared with two twenty litre jerry cans full of diesel. Ronald appeared and carefully placed the plate in front of his loyal customer. "Enjoy!" was all he said, and quickly went back to the kitchen hoping that Terry wouldn't see the big blob of Nutella that was stuck on the underside of the plate after yet another ineffective transit through the dishwasher.

Denzel Sprygelly strode into the Looe River View Hotel and presented himself before his haggard looking nephew. "Good morning young man" Denzel began in his usual condescending manner. "I was hoping we could have a chat."

Paul really didn't have the time. The minibus party which had vacated shortly before, had all been members of the Barking and Dagenham Swingers Society. Paul had first had his suspicions aroused when the booking had been made for the group by one of the TWATS, Alan Badcock. Paul wasn't sure how Badcock fitted in to the picture, but that really wasn't his business. He was in the business of providing accommodation and so Paul had dealt with Badcock's request personally. Badcock had asked for the top floor especially, and even paid for two of the rooms to remain empty.
The group had been well behaved and had kept their activities discreet, or at least that was what Paul had believed until a few moments earlier.

Unfortunately, upon the departure of the guests, the hotel cleaning staff had been horrified to find evidence of some of what had occurred. There were champagne bottles, prosecco bottles, and evidence of spillages in every room. An assortment of underwear also littered the scene. There was blancmange and custard on every surface in one of the rooms. The room next door was full of glitter. The remaining rooms offered things far too horrific to describe here. Suffice to say there was a lot of baby oil, and quite a few wrappers from the types of equipment Marjorie sold. Thick rubber gloves and gallons of sterilising solution were going to be required. The linen would have to be condemned.

Paul had to get the whole floor ready for the next intake of guests at 2pm.
He really didn't have time for Denzel and lifted his head momentarily to say, "Not now Uncle, maybe later? I'm terribly busy at the moment." Denzel carried on anyway.
"I wondered if you could help me with a spot of business?"

Paul ignored his persistent uncle and picked up the phone to ask his friend at a neighbouring hotel if any of the cleaning staff would like a few additional hours this morning. Martin, the friend, was bound to understand. As hoteliers, they had to deal with all sorts of horrors, regularly.
As he hung up the phone, Paul wondered what life would be like as a fisherman. He suffered terribly with seasickness, but it had to be easier than this? Running a hotel was both Emmety, and horrific.

Denzel finally realised that Paul wasn't paying any attention to him. He huffed loudly, as if Paul owed him something, and turned sharply before strutting back outside again. Denzel wasn't accustomed to being treated like this. He made a note to find some way to punish Paul.

Denzel looked up and down the quayside and took in all the little boats the bobbed in the water where fishing boats had once resided. He decided to go to the Social club and see what was going on there today. Perhaps he could find someone in there who'd be willing to hide his intended tracks?

Veryan was about to go off duty when the message from control came through. She made a few notes. Donkey, Hilltop Farm. Could open gates. Might let alpacas out.

She decided she'd better go and investigate. She and Lowenna were on different shifts today. Lowenna had rescheduled herself for late turn for the previous two weeks and was about to start week number three. Lowenna was going to catch the knicker thief if she had to do nights for a year. Lowenna spent good money on her reinforced drawers, and no one was going to get away with stealing them from her.

Veryan smiled at Ronnie and Reggie as they signed in to the pre shift briefing. Veryan quickly updated them, and they decided the missing donkey ought to be a priority. If Ed the Donkey and twenty alpacas were to get loose on the roads, the consequences could be horrible.
They decided to take two cars and go to the location the caller had indicated that Ed might be heading for.

Meanwhile, Ed was enjoying himself. He knew his new human, the one called Adi, loved him. Ed had never been so well looked after. He liked Adi too. He was kind, and he bought ice creams, which Ed happened to rather like. Everyone needed a little variety though, and Ed was enjoying his adventure. His thought process had run along the lines of; visit friends, let friends out of field, all go to beach, all have ice creams, all go back to Adi.

The first two parts of his plan had already been accomplished. Not all of the alpacas had wanted to go to the beach. The lady would be there soon to give them their daily feed of sheep nuts. Most of them though, seventeen

as it happened, thought that following their Donkey friend was a good idea. After all, none of them knew the way.
By the time Veryan and her two colleagues had arrived at Hilltop farm, Ed and his chums were almost at the top of Barbican hill.

Ed had studied the town from his numerous walks with Adi. He didn't much care for cars, they were smelly noisy things, a bit like the children he'd been forced to carry during his slavery days. He selected a route away from the traffic and at the top of Barbican Hill, turned right onto Pendrim Road.
The residents of Elm tree road were speechless as the procession went past, as were the residents on North View.

By the time Veryan, Ronald and Reggie had ushered the three remaining alpacas back into their field, Ed and his friends were emerging onto Fore Street.
Considering it was a bright sunny June day, it was unsurprising the street was full of people.
The alpacas, knowing it was definitely mealtime, and completely unafraid of humans, began to take advantage of all the doors which had been propped open at the shops and cafes.
Looe was used to chaos, but this was an entirely new form of anarchy.

The enticing aroma of food permeated the whole town. The heard began to separate as curious alpacas followed their twitching noses into bakeries and anywhere else they thought they might find a morsel. Startled members of the public dashed fearfully out of the way. One or two of the wetter ones even screamed. The alpacas, not generally known for their aggressive behaviour, ignored the people and rapidly set about consuming whatever they could find.

In the Petrie dish café, Lancelot and Guinevere sniffed at the cake cabinet from behind the counter and decided better of it. Alice and Alonzo were having a great time in the fudge shop and were rapidly clearing the window display. In the bakery, Pedro and Juanita were focussed firmly on the doughnuts. At the door of the small supermarket, Diego, Andrea, and Alejandra tried to navigate the automatic door, but couldn't quite make it through. They decided to cross the road and explore the ice cream shop instead.

Ed, pleased to see his friends were having such a good time, decided to carry on going down the road to the beach. His friends would catch up with him later no doubt, by following his scent. Ed had a mission of his own. Tony had started keeping carrots for him in the workshop recently. Ed loved carrots.

Ronald waved a tea towel at Guinevere and Lancelot in an attempt to shoo them out. Terry looked on in amusement. Ronald had never seen an alpaca before and now the beasts were gone, he turned to Terry to ask him. "What the hell were those things?"
Terry, knowing that Ronald wasn't the brightest spark, took full advantage of the moment. "They'm a cross between the old Cornish cliff goat, and a Bodmin Moor sheep. They call 'em Cornish Scroats."
Ronald accepted this without question. He took out his phone and rang the police control room. Terry had to leave as Ronald tried to explain to the confused call handler that he'd just been invaded by a pair of Cornish Scroats.

Terry managed to contain his laughter until he got to the other side of the road. As he looked around, he noticed there were in fact, Scroats in every direction.

The police control room had received a dozen calls now, some more coherent than others. Some people reported Lamas which confused the issue even more as there was currently a well-publicised gathering of Buddhists who were meditating for peace on a field up beside the monkey sanctuary.
Several members of the public, enjoying the drama immensely, fabricated fantasies of carnage as if the friendly faced alpacas were purposely attacking people, tearing off ears and noses with their ferocious teeth.
When Ronald made his call to report that a group of Scroats were causing mayhem, one of the call handlers had decided to push the panic button. Every available police officer in southeast Cornwall must head for Looe town centre immediately.

Every available police officer in southeast Cornwall consisted of the two patrol cars currently occupied by Veryan, Ronnie and Reggie. Veryan was about to pull out of the driveway to Hilltop farm when Jimmy and Adi appeared. They were both red faced and panting heavily. Adi waved frantically to get Veryan's attention. Veryan paused at the roadside and wound down her window.
"Hi Adi, is the donkey we've been hearing about Ed?"

Looe police had been amused when Adi had begun to take Ed for regular walks. The donkey, no longer a novelty, was really quite popular now, and seeing the pair going for their regular forays to the beach and the woods, had very quickly become just another part of Looe life. Adi had even been taking Ed for a walk when he went to pick up a take-away or pop into the supermarket.

"It is." Adi managed to gasp "Is he here?"

Veryan quickly explained that her colleagues had received several reports now, and that Ed and a group of alpacas, number unknown, were currently exploring the town centre.

"I don't know anything about alpacas" Adi panted "but I'd better get to Ed before he causes any more trouble."

Jimmy, who'd been trailing about 100 yards behind Adi, finally caught up.

"You two had better get in." Veryan indicated the back door of the patrol car.

Denzel hadn't had any success in the social club. All he needed was someone with a small boat to collect a package for him from a yacht that would visit in August.
It was due to arrive on the same day as the annual holiday camp and hotel mascot race. This would be perfect as most people would be distracted by what was happening in the street. He was going to offer two or three of the runners a financial incentive to ensure the distraction was a good one, one which kept his uniformed cousins, Lowenna and Veryan occupied for long enough.

The first part of Denzel's plan had been to borrow the Lenny the Lugworm suit. He decided he'd have to re-think that, given Pauls rudeness and lack of cooperation.
The second part was the collection itself. As long as he was handed his package somewhere in the town, he reckoned he would be able to conceal it quickly enough to avoid detection. The risky part was the journey from the Dutchman's yacht to the shore. Consequently, Denzel needed a boat.

Denzel crossed the road and lent on the railings absently gazing across the water. He wondered what all the screaming was about. A blue flashing light attracted his attention as a police car drove down Barbican Hill. Another pulled onto Fore Street from the bridge. Denzel said a short prayer to the Norse god Loki that the police cars weren't going anywhere near any of his interests.
If he'd continued looking across the river, he'd have spotted the four alpacas that were now investigating the Harbour Café. His attention was caught by something else though, a familiar sound from years gone by. There in the middle of the river, proudly taking his latest acquisition out for a test run, was Ryan Smugly in a beautifully lacquered

Doodlebug.
That would do nicely Denzel thought, rubbing his hands together in anticipation. Better still, when it came to Smugly, Denzel had leverage.
He might not make it into the TWATS officially this year, but he was definitely in most of the other games in town. He decided to go and have a drink while he planned how to best manipulate the TWATS. He was going to be able to use them after all. Denzel loved having power over people.

Oblivious to the pandemonium across the bridge, Denzel climbed into his Smart car, and drove out to the tennis club bar opposite the island. He deliberately parked right opposite the coastguard station. The more his car was seen, the less it would be noticed he reasoned, soon it would just become another part of the background and despite the livid colour, would barely register in the minds of the people who saw it. Denzel had learned a lot in prison.

In the bar, he ordered himself a cocktail and went to sit at a table which offered him a view of the bay across to Rame Head. He'd distrusted the Dutchman when the stranger had first approached him, but the man had offered him 'Two kilos of Columbia's finest' when they'd met a few days earlier.

The Dutchman had simply said that he was a friend of many friends and had proceeded to shake Denzel's hand in a manner known only to members of the closest inner circles.

There had been several incidents of handshaking lately. His meeting with the TWATS had been one such episode. He noticed they all used the same handshake as the Dutchman

too. Denzel could only assume that the gang of four were 'Brothers' from a different branch of the Special Club, St Austell perhaps?
Afterwards Denzel had felt an overwhelming urge to go and wash his hands. The TWATS were even more slippery than the people he'd met in prison. Then again, of course they were, that's why they were all still outside.
Dobson hadn't wanted to shake his hand at all. John Dory had growled under his breath "Shake it lad". As usual, Dobson had done as he was told.

This new proposal by the Dutchman was an entirely new venture for Denzel, he dreamt of bundles of fifty-pound notes.

His previous foray into drug dealing had been getting all his elderly relatives to ask for as much on prescription as they could. Every one of the Sprygelly family, had given up smoking at least five or six times apparently, and Denzel had made a modest profit selling nicotine patches.
He expected this latest venture would run along much the same lines, and he'd probably deal with the same customers.
Of course, he wouldn't get his hands dirty with anything as seedy as distribution. He'd find a young, vulnerable user for that, and then manipulate him or even better, her.
A pretty girl, he thought, that would be perfect. She could flit from bar to bar and party to party. A young, keen social butterfly. Someone well liked and who'd display sufficient flesh to blind people to what was really going on.
Someone who could keep her mouth shut when she inevitably got arrested, and then eventually give her captors the completely untrue, unprovable story he intended to create as to where the drugs had come from. Someone he

could trust. He started to run through a list of his nieces.

He rather liked the idea of making Dobson the main supplier in the story. It would be a great laugh watching the drugs squad tear Dobson's house apart. Denzel chuckled to himself as he pictured the scene. It didn't matter that the chosen niece would probably end up in prison herself, Denzel had plenty of nieces.
He might just send the Drugs squad some anonymous tips about Dobson anyway.
Then he thought about Smugly and the Doodlebug. That could be woven into a good story too.
Denzel had no idea that Smugly had bought the little boat for exactly that reason.
Denzel decided to congratulate himself with another cocktail.

As Denzel revelled in self-praise, Ryan Smugly was returning to the harbour. He'd spotted Cowboy and that other weirdo in their own Doodlebug as he'd headed eastward for a test run to Cawsand.

On his return, he was surprised to see the pair still on the water, gradually heading further out to sea now. It didn't take smugly long to work out they were in trouble. The weirdo, what was his name again? Oh yes, Keith the flasher, was clearly blue with cold.

A poorly prepared seagoer could easily die from exposure out here.

Smugly could have puttered over and towed the other boat back in. That would have meant some effort on his part though, not to mention fuel. He carried on his way back in past the Banjo pier and fished out his phone to call the RNLI.

In the town centre, the alpacas were having a lovely time. The owner had finally been contacted and Radio Cornwall had been urged to put out a call for anyone with a horsebox, to ask if they'd come to help gather up the cheerful animals. There were now around thirty land rovers with horseboxes blocking the Quay, the main road, and the carpark.

The round up was a slow process. Most of the alpacas had feasted on a variety of sugary substances. Juan and Juanita, unlike their British namesakes, had even tried a few vegetarian pasties.

Volunteers closed in on alpacas, alpacas evaded capture and trotted away another few feet, all the while smiling. And so, the pantomime continued, for hours.

Most of the shops had closed their doors now. Inside, major clean-up operations were underway. In the Petrie

Dish café Ronald had swept up some droppings with a dustpan and given the cake cabinet a quick wipe with one of his famous filthy cloths. That would do until the morning he thought as he locked up for the night. It was the most thorough clean the place had had in months.

Ed the donkey had been happy to see Adi. He'd enjoyed his adventure. He'd seen his friends, and he'd had ice cream direct from the tub in one of the cafes on the seafront, at least until the owner had ushered him outside again. Tony wasn't working on a Saturday; he was far too sensible for that. One of his colleagues was on duty and was currently picking litter off the beach. The colleague had left the workshop door open just a couple of inches. It wasn't long before clever Ed had nudged it open and successfully located Tony's carrot stash. He was still munching when Adi appeared.
"Oh mate, what have you done?" Adi took a step towards his four-legged friend.
Ed didn't understand what was being said but responded in donkey anyway. "Hello nice friend, I've had a lovely time, look, carrots, would you like some?"
Adi took Ed by the collar he always wore and gently urged him towards the door. "Come on mate, we need to get you home. I think we both might be in a world of trouble"
Ed, compliantly went in the direction Adi was leading him. It was obviously home time. What a great day he'd had. He'd have to do it again!

Veryan regretted having stayed on now. She could have gone off duty at 2pm and spared herself all this. On the brighter side, although she'd done her best to retain a respectable gravity while handling the situation, most of the shenanigans were hysterical. It was certainly a lot more entertaining than most Saturdays. Mike had closed his shop and had joined the spectators. He brought out cups of tea for Veryan and the other two uniformed police officers.

What had left Veryan rather puzzled, was a number of plain closed bystanders, who had come forward and discreetly identified themselves as police officers too. They had then joined in with the effort to contain the alpacas. There were at least ten of them. Veryan recognised a few of the faces and realised these were people new to the town who she'd been seeing regularly for several weeks now.
Clearly, something big was happening in the town and she and Lowenna knew nothing about it
The last time Looe had seen that many, obviously on duty police officers, was when Prince Charles had come to visit.

By 6pm, Adi had arrived back at home and put Ed into his little stable for the night.
His neighbours had given up trying to erect the tunnel and a party had developed. Adi accepted their invitation to join them.

The barbecue had been lit and someone had produced a pile of sausages and buns. Rachael was anxious to know where her Jimmy was. "I hope he's not too tired." she confided in Adi, who was salivating at the barbecue aroma. "I've got plans for him when he gets back."
Adi gratefully accepted a pair of hotdogs and hoped she meant plans to feed him.

Marjorie and Sylvia were clearly plastered, as was Eileen. There were whoops of laughter that could be heard all the way up the valley. Donald and Norman appeared to be sharing a joint. Alan, who'd had a puff on the joint also, had gone inside to change out of his overalls and put something a bit more practical on. No one was surprised when he reappeared carrying a case of bottles of cider and wearing the wizard outfit.

Lowenna came on duty at 10pm. She'd decided not to wear her sergeant's tunic this evening, instead she'd opted for her running gear. Lowenna could move surprisingly quickly when the need arose. Right now, she was feeling especially motivated.

Looking at the call logs, it looked as if Saturday nights had been busy ones for the knicker thief. It made sense, there were so many ridiculous drink related incidents on a Saturday, most people just ignored the noises and comings and goings of the participants.
Usually, Lowenna and her team had to cover the entire area with just two cars. It was impossible to cover everywhere and attend every incident. Inevitably, people were getting away with things.

Lowenna knew that some aspects of the town were wonderful.
There were so many decent, honest hard-working people, it warmed Lowenna's heart when she thought of some of the kindnesses.
It was those good people who she felt she was serving. People like Lewis, the man who'd always kept a box of fish on the quay so that visiting children could feed the seal. Then there was the lovely lady who used to work at the school, Peggy. She always had a kind word, a cheerful smile, and a beautiful twinkle in her eye. Everyone loved her, and when news of her passing spread through the community, far more tears were shed than her family would have thought possible. She had been loved and would be greatly missed.
Steve the postman was known as the nicest man in Royal Mail, and justifiably. He'd be terribly missed when he retired. He'd given years of his life in service to the town,

and he was respected and well liked, and in Lowenna's mind, quite rightly so.

The Lions did a great job, one of the former mayors could often be seen collecting litter from the roadsides, and several years before, a group of locals had worked incredibly hard to create a festival for the town.

All these were the warm hearted, generous people who gave so much of themselves to benefit the town.

Then there was the other side. The seedy, slimy underbelly. The people who schemed and plotted and dealt in whispers and back-handers. There was blatant nepotism, and the Dodgy-favour-bank did more business than the financial one.

If the true scale of the law breaking had been uncovered, people would be horrified. It started with bending a few rules and ended up in corruption on a scale that Lowenna could have wept about.

A lot of it was things she couldn't do anything about, things like the life endangering hygiene in the Petrie Dish café. Mark Wray was keeping busy trying to sort out the employment and exploitation problems. Elsewhere, all sorts of other problems existed. Negligent landlords, selfish aggressive next-door neighbours, casual acts of vandalism. All this was outside of Lowenna's remit. Although, with her martial arts training, she was quite good at restraining some of the idiots when their behaviour spilled over sufficiently to warrant intervention. Sometimes she might accidentally drop one of said idiots down a flight of steps.

Tonight, Lowenna was determined she was going to find the knicker thief if he was active. And before he was locked up for the night, Lowenna was going to introduce him to

the presence of certain pressure points.
How bloody dare he!
Lowenna simmered as she prepared herself for the evening.

She was using her own car this evening. Her colleagues would no doubt be kept busy in the marked cars. She'd drafted in some extra bodies on the grounds that five of the alpacas were still unaccounted for. She'd also sent out a text message to all her family members to text her instantly if they detected anything unusual occurring in their own, or any of their neighbours' gardens.

By midnight, Lowenna had received so many texts from her family, that even with her vast experience, she was dumbstruck by some of the messages she received. The vast majority were nothing she wanted to involve herself with, but the range of activities was truly staggering. Lowenna quickly began to regret having asked her friends and family to text her.

One cousin wanted to make a formal complaint that some of her friends hadn't sent her any birthday cards.
Another wanted Lowenna to attend his property as a particularly pestiferous badger kept rummaging through his dustbins.
At Emmety Villa, there was clearly a party and barbecue going on. Lowenna wasn't sure what law was being broken by a few of her cousins and a few new residents enjoying themselves in the privacy of their own property.
Her phone beeped again. This time, a niece had seen her ex-boyfriend, from about two years previously, on the seafront apparently, skinny dipping with another girl.
The text messages continued. Cousin Gerren reported scratching in his loft. He suspected it was squirrels.

There was a swinger's party going on at Alan Badcock's house. Cousin Laura and her husband knew this for certain. They had taken a ladder round to next door and then taken it in turns confirming the identities of the participants. Derek had almost fallen off the ladder while he'd been writing down the names.
At Woodlands View, someone had stolen a garden gnome painted in Manchester City colours. The owner, who wished to remain anonymous, had been receiving ransom notes and photos of his precious gnome perched on bars and counter tops all over the town. Lowenna recognised the number of the cousin who'd sent that one in and had to laugh. The cousin in question took his football extremely seriously. The ransom notes were being sent by his wife.
It had been Lowenna's idea.

Veryan had sent a message. She'd lost two pairs of silkies this afternoon. Veryan was deeply unhappy.

Between text messages from her family, Lowenna moved around the different vantage points in the town and scanned the area with her night vision binoculars. At just after midnight, she was rewarded for her determination when she spotted a tall slim figure behaving strangely at the top of Portbyhan Road. She'd been parked on Pendrim Road on the other side of the river when she'd spied him. She climbed back into her car and made her way over to the Downs.

Her police radio was on, so she knew her uniformed colleagues were busy dealing with a group of youths who'd attempted to ram-raid a newsagents in Liskeard. They had probably been after cigarettes. It had been a poor choice; the newsagents had closed some twelve months previously

and the building was scheduled for demolition.
All the youths had succeeded in doing was wedging their stolen Nissan micra into the doorway so that they couldn't open its doors. It had provided some comic relief to the officers from dealing with the usual Saturday night oafs.

Unfortunately, by the time Lowenna had arrived at the top of Portbyhan Road, there was no sign of anyone. It was just then that Lowenna's phone beeped again. It was her husband this time. He'd been just about to go to bed and so he'd let the cat out. The single pair of apple catchers Lowenna had left on the line at the rear of her house as bait, had vanished.
Lowenna drove out to a quiet lane by Trelawne woods and let out a long, anguished scream. She was incandescent.

Lowenna took her flask from the back seat and poured herself a mug of tea. It was almost an hour before she felt sufficiently calm to be able to drive safely again.
She decided to drive back into town and complete another circuit. It was only twenty past one, and the need for her presence in the main town wouldn't begin until the late bars and discotheques began to empty inebriated punters onto the streets.

She drove out to Hannafore first. She spotted Cousin Denzel's banana yellow Smart car still parked by the tennis club. There was no sign of Denzel himself. She wondered again whether Denzel might be her target after all.

Denzel as it happened, was tucked up in bed at home. The barman had ordered him a taxi when, after his eleventh cocktail, Denzel had decided to start singing Cornish songs. 'Cousin Jack' and 'This is my Cornwall' were no problem, but when he'd started his rendition of 'Kiss-chase with my cousins', the owner had decided it was time for him to leave.

Lowenna completed her circuit and was just going back around by the fire station, when she saw a familiar figure emerging from the bottom of North Road. There was no denying it was him, even in this light, he looked as if his head was on wrong. Bill Dobson looked straight at Lowenna. He looked guilty. That didn't mean anything though. In Lowenna's experience, Dobson looked guilty most of the time. He was wearing running gear. Remembering the figure she'd spotted at the top of Portbyhan Road, she quickly brought the car to a stop beside Dobson as he tried to slip away behind the Spar shop.
She climbed out onto the road to intercept him.
"You're out late Bill, do you need a lift?"
Dobson stopped alongside Lowenna's car.
"That's kind, but I'm getting into training again, you know, next year's ten miler" Dobson replied mentioning the annual ten-mile event. It was known as hilly and hellish, and not for the faint hearted.
Lowenna looked at her watch and then asked, "It's a bit late Bill, how come you're out at this hour?"
"Oh, you know" he blustered, "I've been pretty nocturnal ever since I worked in the bakery."
Lowenna knew this wasn't true. Dobson lived just around the corner from her, and she did enough circuits of the town when she was on duty to have a realistic notion of his movements.
She decided not to press the point. Over the next few nights though, she'd be keeping an eye on Dobson.
"Ah, okay then, goodnight Bill."

Lowenna climbed bag into her car and headed towards the bridge. Could Dobson be the one?
She'd noted the trainers he'd been wearing, Dobson had big feet, at least a size twelve she reckoned. She decided to drive up to her house. She'd left a covering of sand in several places in her garden, including beneath her washing line.
She needed to go and check for footprints.

Lowenna was just about to turn into the top of Sunrising when she spotted another familiar figure. She had no difficulty recognising Alan Badcock. Strangely, he was dressed in running gear too. Hadn't her cousin said that Badcock had a full swingers party underway? What was he up to she wondered? Before she could stop her car again, Badcock had disappeared into the alleyway that led down to the playschool. Be the time Lowenna had driven to the other end of the alleyway, Badcock had vanished into the night.

Lowenna did not make it home until several hours later. Calls had begun to come through on her police radio and she spent the rest of the night shift dealing with drunks and the recipients of their assorted palavers.
The extra officers she'd called in were a godsend, if only she could have those numbers every week. The numbers of uniforms present had caused a significant drop in the number of fights and drink driving incidents. There hadn't been any calls about vandalism either. They'd even managed to re-capture another two alpacas.

What there had been were several arrests for public urination. Lowenna could use this information to petition the town council to leave at least one of the public toilets open, once it had been made vandal-proof of course. Dismayed shop owners regularly had to deal with this on Sunday mornings. It just wasn't fair. The bar owners made a profit, and the shopkeepers had to clean up the filth. The town council repeatedly failed to acknowledge the issue. It was just one of their several blind spots.

Predictably, a scuffle had broken out at the taxi rank, and another at the Kebab shop. These had been dealt with swiftly too. Everyone involved was formally arrested and charged. For once, a few of these idiots would have to go to court. Lowenna was pleased. It would set an example to some of the others who were beginning to think of themselves as untouchable.

Best of all, was the revelation that a squad of under-cover plain clothes police had also been in the town that night. Lowenna hadn't known a thing.
At least half a dozen drug dealers had been arrested over the course of the evening it transpired and taken straight

into Plymouth for intense questioning.
Lowenna was delighted to learn that one of them was the older guy who she had suspected of supplying hard drugs to fourteen-year old's on the seafront.

The only thing which had been out of the ordinary was that Uncle Keith hadn't shown up anywhere. Uncle Keith hadn't been picked up for weeks. That was definitely a turn up for the books, or as Ronald would have said, "Some fink you put in your diary"

At last, the paperwork was done, and Lowenna could go home.
The town routine began all over again as the first of the street cleaners began to deal with bottles and chip wrappers and stolen pint glasses half full of lager.

At Emmety Villa, Rachael was finally allowing Jimmy to get some sleep.

Norman and Sylvia were asleep in their chairs next to the barbecue. Donald and Marjorie had made it back inside to their beds.

Alan and Eileen were inside too. Eileen had put on her witches' outfit for Alan and the pair were now lying contentedly in one another's arms. They were both drooling.

Denzel had been woken by the first of the gulls and was crawling through to his bathroom in search of something to alleviate the pain in his skull.

Paul Sprygelly was drinking coffee in order to get through

yet another busy breakfast in the Looe River View Hotel.

Cowboy and Uncle Keith had been drinking salvaged vodka all night and were now in a similar position to Alan and Eileen.

The sun rose higher, and the sound of gulls gradually faded as thousands flew inland for a day of pillaging whatever they could find away from the coast.

In Plymouth, DI Bernard Flood examined the pages of useful information that had been acquired as a result of last night's pull. He was pleased. It was time the lovely little town was cleaned up a bit, and although he knew he'd never get them all, he was certain that soon enough, he'd be lifting quite a few people who should have been picked up years before.
It was a shame he couldn't get them for all their crimes. People like Denzel Sprygelly for instance, and John Dory and his mate Smugly.
He'd get them for something though. Flood had put a lot of hours into his intended bust, and it would send out shockwaves in the rest of the community. Flood intended to retire to Looe, and before he did, he planned to clean some of the filth off the streets.

# July.

The holiday season was fully underway. Lowenna had been sitting at her desk looking at personal CCTV systems. She still didn't know who the thief was, and she'd lost another three pairs of bait. The thefts had continued, and over a wider area now. Whoever it was had begun to operate in the villages too.
Veryan had made an interesting observation. She'd been reading about the One hundred Monkeys experiment conducted by Japanese scientists. Perhaps the same thing was going on here she pondered? Perhaps once a certain number of knicker thieves lived in an area, other people spontaneously began to mimic the same behaviour? Lowenna thought it unlikely.

Her perusal of security systems was interrupted when Veryan called her through to the room where the police officers kept their kettle.
"Oh my god Low'" she called, using her cousins familiar name. "You've got to see this lot. If this isn't hundred monkeys, I don't know what is."
At the little railway station, the twin carriage train was disgorging visitors onto the platform. As the brightly coloured mass of humanity spewed out onto the pavement, Lowenna began to realise what her cousin had been referring to. It was as if the cast of the Lion king had come to visit. Animal print leggings were an incredibly popular choice. In a throwback to big haired 80's rock music, some of the men were wearing them too.

The pair looked on in voyeuristic fascination as the parade went by.

"Leopard, leopard, tiger, another leopard, Oo look, a zebra. Tiger, leopard, is that a giraffe?" Veryan pointed through the mirrored glass.
Lowenna picked up where Veryan had left off. "Tiger, another tiger, blue leopard."
"I can see another zebra" Veryan chipped in as they both warmed to the game.
"I think the leopards have it." Lowenna carried on looking. "Leopard, tiger, tiger, leopard, tiger, is that a gazelle? And what's that one?" Before Veryan could answer, Lowenna finished the sentence and then let her mouth hang open. "You've got to be kidding me! Is that supposed to be a Rhinoceros?"
Gradually the procession disappeared as it headed down the road in the general direction of the beach.
A few Impala and wildebeest brought up the rear.

"How about animal bingo?" Veryan suggested to her Sargent. "Oh, go on then." Lowenna answered laughing. They both knew it was highly inappropriate, but in their job, they'd grasp at whatever it took to help get them through the day.
"I'll make some bingo cards later." Veryan said as she handed Lowenna a freshly made cup of coffee.
"Winner on ten cards then?" Lowenna suggested and added "Loser buys the wine?"
"You're on" her cousin answered brightly.
The town buzzed with noises of summer. The gulls called constantly. In the main streets, children who had been forcibly removed from shops howled in protest.
"I've told you you're not having it Bentley." And. "No Aluna, you've already spent all your money." Could be heard emanating from stressed parents as their offspring screamed in protest. The harassed parents would manage to

drag their manipulative children almost twenty yards along the busy main road before collapsing and taking the bawling offspring back to the same shops they'd just been dragged out of, where they were then rewarded for their appalling behaviour.

At the pedestrian crossing on the bridge, a confrontation had developed between local girl, Helen, and the driver of a Gobi Desert patrol wagon. The driver of the tank had almost run into Helen as she'd legitimately attempted to cross the road on a red light.
Helen was struggling with the increasing rudeness of some of the visitors, and almost being run over hadn't done much to improve her morning.
"For god's sake, slow down will you." She'd snapped through the open passenger window.
"I wasn't going fast" the driver snapped back, "and anyway, what a stupid place for a crossing." As if he thought that made his behaviour any more acceptable. He was obviously impressed with himself and, ignoring the traffic building up behind him now the lights had turned to green again added. "I don't know what's wrong with you people, we come down here and spend our money."
Helen was already finding summer stressful, but to have this twerp attempt to harangue her now, was the final pulling of the pin from the grenade. She stepped up to the window of the vehicle and fixed the mouthy driver with a Medusa like stare.
"Oh, we like taking your money" She said icily "and then we like it even better when you finally fuck off home."
The driver was momentarily speechless. Helen didn't give him a chance to answer. Taking in his glaring attire of pink lycra vest top and bright orange fake tan, she added. "Do you know what we call you? We call you the FFF's, the fat

fluorescent fuckers." She was on a roll now.
"You'd better be on your way pal, before Jimmy Saville's family come looking for his trackie bottoms."
With that, she smartly turned and continued on her way. It had been like releasing the valve on a pressure cooker. For the rest of the day, Helen was as serene as an angel.

Norman and Marjorie were trying to make their way down the street. They'd planned to meet Donald and Sylvia in the nice pub in the centre of town, the one with the coal fire. Norman kept muttering under his breath. "God these people are tedious, do they really have to waddle six abreast and at a snail's pace?" Norman wasn't particularly fit and agile these days, although the cannabis did help. Compared to this lot though, he was positively dynamic. Marjorie wasn't impressed either. "Oh, these flaming people. Surely, they can't all be on holiday? Look at them, they never stop eating. It's no wonder they're all so unhealthy. I hope that wall can hold up to that." She indicated the thick low granite wall that ran alongside the carpark. A family of assorted African and Indian big cats was accompanied by a zebra and a hippopotamus who were greedily stuffing chips into their mouths.
Norman and Marjorie hadn't lost their accents, but in the seven short weeks since they'd moved into Emmety Villa, they'd already adopted a great many of the local customs. Grumbling about the visitors was one of them.

Donald and Sylvia were only just down the road. Two or three minutes in September, anything up to twenty in July and August. Donald had been hoping to catch Cowboy and Uncle Keith lurking in their usual haunt. He wanted some more of the blue pills. Cowboy, while pretending to work at Emmety Villa, had guaranteed he could get more. He kept changing the date. Donald had been forced to pay pharmacy prices, and he didn't like that. He and Sylvia had decided they might try some of the white pills again too if they were available. Donald in particular had thought a bit more dancing might be a particularly good idea, just like Paul Sprygelly, he'd put on quite a lot of weight since Easter.

Donald had been reading the notices posted by the TWATS while Sylvia nipped to the loo. There was a lot going on. The TWATS owned most of the paid car parking spaces in the town and the Park and Ride at the end of Barbican. They owned the West Top field, where it was proposed the long-desired supermarket would be built. They owned several shops, and the tourist information building was theirs too; they rented that one to the town council for a hugely inflated fee. Considering the TWATS existed to support the town, they were particularly efficient at extracting money from it, money far and above what they needed to maintain their little empire.

Mark Wray was about to enter the TWATS office. Donald recognised him from his stay in the Looe River View Hotel. He'd thought he was one of the managers. "Good morning." Donald offered.

"Good morning." Mark replied. He didn't know the man, but he was always polite, and he met so many people anyway, that they'd probably been introduced at some time.

Mark had work to do. He pushed the door to the office open and stepped inside.

He knew the TWATS had been preparing for him, so he knew he'd have to uncover their false accounting. Mark was going to enjoy this.

Still on the street, Donald and Sylvia had stopped to enjoy a busker. The busker was dressed in green and had made himself look every inch a Leprechaun. Donald dropped a few coins into the guitar case and smiled at the Leprechaun. The Leprechaun scowled back at him. Clearly the Leprechaun was having a bad day. He finished singing 'Dirty Old Town' and began the mournful chords of 'Heaven knows I'm miserable now.'

Donald, uninhibited, sang along with the opening verse and at the words "I was looking for a job and then I found a job, and heaven knows I'm miserable now" burst out laughing.

The Leprechaun was clearly even less happy than when he'd begun.

On the quay, Jimmy and Rachael loaded a picnic into their little Doodlebug. They were going to Lantic Bay for the day. It was their favourite beach, and rightly so. Challenging to get to, a boat was the ideal way. It was beautiful, and at times, very private. Rachael's plans didn't end at sunbathing.

Denzel watched as Jimmy and Rachael untied their mooring rope and began a careful exit of the harbour. Denzel needed a boat, and it looked like his niece Rachael, had just what he needed.

At Emmety Villa, Alan, predictably wearing the wizard outfit, was working on his business plan. He'd need rent for two years; he'd need the stock. He'd have to learn to use a sewing machine, or perhaps find a seamstress locally. He'd need a sign and advertising. He'd also need to budget for all his utilities.

He sighed as he looked through his calculations again. Eileen came over to him and affectionately stroked the

back of his head. "How does it look love?" She asked.
"I think we'd need about £60'000, but we'd probably start to make money back from day one if we do it here in Looe." He answered, "But where on earth do we get the money?"
Eileen had been researching too. "I found us some money spells darling" she smiled "Let's get up in the woods tonight, it's a new moon."
Alan got onto his feet and hugged his wife. They made a wonderful team, she never failed to support him, and he did his best to look after her too.
It was decided then, they would use magic.

# August.

Lowenna and Veryan discussed the plan for tomorrow. It was the Looe Holiday Camp and Hotel mascot annual fun run day. They would both be on duty, and as the heavy suits of the participants meant that running in them was virtually impossible anyway, decided to accompany the entrants as they progressed along the route.
Their colleagues could deal with the traffic management aspects this time. Lowenna and Veryan wanted to be on the scene.

Veryan had a list of names of the runners. There would be a lot of children around and the camps didn't always have the most up to date information on their employees. They'd decided to make a quick check on their own database. Veryan read the names as Lowenna scrolled through the records on her computer.
"Dan Gleeballs" she announced and then chortled. "Oh, the poor lad, that's Cousin Jago's boy isn't it?"
Lowenna chuckled and checked the name.
"He's a goodun. I'm glad, I've always like Dan Gleeballs" she answered with a broad grin. "Next?"
"No first name, this one is our porpoise apparently, Mr P. Nurse." Lowenna turned and gave Veryan a cryptic stare.
"No, really" Veryan continued earnestly, nodding.
Lowenna typed the name in the search bar, it came back with an NHI, 'No information held', response. "Next" she called.
"Jenny Taylor." Lowenna turned fully in her seat this time.
"I'm not making it up." Veryan protested "These are the names I was given."
"Hmmm" was all Lowenna responded now, and she

tapped in the name to get another NIH.
And thus, it went on for the next half hour.
Mr G. Raff. Mike Oxlong, and more in the same vein. At last, they came to the final name on the list, a local girl, a cousin, and someone they both knew well, Polly Dactyl. Polly would be wearing an Octopus costume.

At Emmety Villa, Cousin Rachael was still in bed. Jimmy had just come back from the bathroom and was getting ready for work. He'd changed all the schedules recently so that everyone took a turn at early mornings, late nights and weekends. Previously there had been so much favouritism that recruiting was a constant feature. Good people had kept coming and then promptly leaving again. Since evening things out, he had a much more balanced and happier workforce. He certainly needed that; the six weeks of high summer were intense. His regular entanglements with Rachael also helped his stress levels.

She was trying to lure him back into the bed as he dressed. She tugged at the edge of his towel as he sat on the bed to put on his socks. "Go on Jimmy, do woo-woo for me? I want to see pant hamster again."
"I'd love to my darling, but there's bound to be half a dozen drama's I'll have to sort out. I need to get on."

Just last night at work, Jimmy had needed to intervene when a woman in her late thirties had run out of patience with her husband and begun flinging packets of hot dog rolls at him down the length of one of the aisles. There had been shouting and screaming, and then she'd run out of hot-dog buns and decided to use ketchup. Luckily, Jimmy had used his new assertiveness to put a very abrupt stop to things.

He'd even persuaded her to put the hot-dog buns back, rather than find herself introduced to Looe's uniformed branch.

This was only one of a dozen similar incidents daily at the moment. He knew that every year, they'd have at least one 'Big one' a week during the summer. They hadn't had one yet this week. He'd better get down there before things kicked off.

"I have to check the boat too you know, it's big tides at the moment and she's riding high in the water. I need to adjust the lines."
"You can ride my waves if you like." She pulled back the covers to reveal an expanse of slightly hairy, snow-white flesh."
"I have to get on darling." Jimmy reiterated jerking a thumb at the alarm clock. It was almost 11am and he had to be there for Noon.
Rachael gave a disappointed sigh and then smiled at him. "I'm making a booking for later then. I've got a delivery due from Marjorie later."
"Oh, erm, great." Was all Jimmy could say. Rachael had introduced him to a whole new world, but some of the things she'd ordered really hadn't held an appeal for him. He'd learned about something called Pegging recently. He sincerely hoped that Rachael hadn't.

Cowboy and Uncle Keith were on the quay making sure the Doodlebug was ready and full of diesel this time. Cowboy was excited. He was telling Keith what the Dutchman had told him on the phone the night before. "He said he had as much as we want, any fink up to fifty grand!"

Keith was delighted. "How much have we got?"
Between them, the pair had managed to scrape just over thirty thousand pounds together.
There were the original bags of pills, the sea gifted vodka, both of them had produced their life savings from their hiding places, and they'd also been running a scam giving visitors boat rides to Polperro.

Keith would go to Polperro on the bus. Cowboy would take half a dozen visitors to the village by sea and drop them off for an hour.
When the visitors got back to the little boat, Keith would declare that the other guy had been forced to go home due to an emergency. He could take the visitors back of course, but it would be an extra trip as he had his own group to pick up, so they'd have to pay for the return trip, again.
The visitors wouldn't realise it was the same boat, and the pair would change the steering wheel cover from a red one to a blue one, hiding the spare in the central locker.
Back in Looe, Keith would pick up a new group and then swap with Cowboy when he got back to the village again. Every passenger paid twice for a trip on the same boat, all the while uninsured, and crewed by amateurs.

"We could do wiv some more dosh really." Cowboy huffed.

The stakes in this game were getting much higher than he'd ever expected. The depths he was willing to stoop to were no lower than anyone who knew him would have been surprised by.
"I'll give it some thought." he finished.

Denzel was facing the same dilemma. The Dutchman had

just rung to confirm tomorrow afternoons drop off.
The bay would be full of boats and inflatables, kayakers and windsurfers, the perfect cover.
The original deal was for a single two kilo package, now he was being offered pills and even more of Columbia's finest. Anything up to a hundred thousand the Dutch accented voice on the other end of the line had said.

Denzel did have that much in cash stashed away, that and considerably more in fact, but his highly tuned rat senses were telling him not to use his own money. He thought about it.
He had plenty of leverage where the TWATS were concerned.
They were under extreme pressure at the moment anyway. Mark Wray's investigation had led to him calling in the charities commission inspectors. Denzel knew the gang of four principal TWATS were sweating.
Denzel also knew that pressurised people were vulnerable people. It was time for a little blackmail then.

DI Bernard Flood had just one more call to make on the marine telephone that sat on his desk in the drug squad office in Plymouth. He was working with Customs and Excise now, and they'd given him some surprising information on Ryan Smugly.

Smugly had been one of theirs once. He'd taken early retirement after a disciplinary case was raised against him. There were allegations Smugly had stolen personal items, underwear in fact, from the lockers of his female colleagues. Smugly had also been implicated in something else.
Money confiscated during operations was unaccounted for. Smugly had clearly been living far beyond his means. He and his wife both drove expensive cars. They owned several properties, and he took additional unpaid leave up to four times a year for expensive foreign holidays.
The subsequent investigation hadn't been able to determine how exactly Smugly had laundered the money, and so he was never charged.
Flood had known he was a wrong-un the first time he'd set eyes on him. His coppers nose was rarely wrong. His tweed jacket and marmite voice had only served to make Flood even more suspicious.

Smugly had disappeared to Spain for several years, only to reappear in Looe in the 1990's claiming he was an ex-Royal Navy officer.
Since then, he'd sat on an assortment of committees. His personality profiles had said he was an insecure individual who held a deeply seated desire to be important and looked up to.
Now he was chief of the TWATS.
Also, apparently, he was willing to trade in filth that would

poison the very community he pretended to be such a pillar of.

Flood had specialised in catching bottom feeders like Smugly, Cowboy and Sprygelly for his whole career. Flood, unknown to his colleagues, had connections to Looe too. It was why he wanted to retire there.
The work was done, the scene was set. Two dozen of his best officers had tracked his targets movements for months.

Cowboy had done a job repairing a flat roof for Floods Auntie Alice once. He'd charged her three times the going rate for the job, and the very next storm, had taken the whole thing away. Alice had needed to stay with friends and pay all over again to get the roof fixed properly. While she was away, Cowboy had gone back and stolen shrubs and daffodil bulbs which he'd then planted in his own garden.
That idiot known as Uncle Keith had flashed at the same auntie several times. She wasn't in any danger sexually but seeing his little maggot had made her laugh so much, she was in danger of having another asthma attack.

Lastly, there was Denzel Sprygelly. Master manipulator, dishonest Denzel. there was no depth he wouldn't stoop to if it meant making a profit.
Denzel's first ever business had been selling ice creams from a small cabin on the seafront. He was seventeen and brawny.
It wasn't long until he'd acquired enough money to pay someone else to do the serving.
Sprygelly would wait until small children came up to the kiosk without their parents. The employee, usually one of

Sprygellys cousins, would serve the children and take the money.
Sprygelly would then either take the cones off the children by force, or spit on them.
Then he'd disappear for a few minutes.
The children would go running back to their horrified parents, crying.
The parents would go straight back to the kiosk and buy their distressed children fresh ice creams.
Denzel would snigger from his vantage point by the alleyway by the library.
He sold a lot more ice creams that way. He kept it up all summer.
One little boy had the misfortune to have his ice cream stolen three times in a week.
That little boy was Chris, the driver. His father was DI Bernard Flood.

Flood had family connections with Looe going back further than Sprygelly himself. Flood had garnered all sorts of little gems about Sprygelly on the family gossip line over the years. Sprygelly had lied, stolen, cheated and bullied a great many of Floods family over the last four decades.

Bernard Flood was looking forward to handcuffing this lot tomorrow, especially Denzel Sprygelly. It was just a shame Flood thought, that Dobson, Badcock and Dory wouldn't also be there tomorrow. He had enough on them to put them away too.

Phones had been tapped, photographs taken, so had an assortment of witness statements, discreetly of course.
 No one liked the TWATS, or Denzel, or Cowboy and Uncle Keith for that matter.

Flood laughed, they'd all already convicted themselves, now all he had to do was prove intent. As soon as he'd handed over the packets, and money had changed hands, the game was over.

He laughed again. The packets didn't even contain anything illicit. He substituted pills for chalk tablets usually used as placebos in drug trials.
And Columbia's finest? To make things appear the correct weight, Bernard's team had taped up packets of coffee beans. They were exactly as described.

In the garden at Emmety Villa, Donald and Norman were busy potting up cannabis plants. The cuttings they had grown had developed healthy root systems and were now almost twelve inches tall. They were ready to be transferred to the final receptacles. Donald and Norman carefully interspersed them between the tomato plants and the butternut squash vines they'd started in June. It was late in the season, but with any luck, September would be mild, and they could gather in the harvest at the end of October. They wanted to get finished today. Tomorrow was fun run day and they'd decided to join the festivities.

Ed was trying to get their attention by the fence which separated his patch of field on the plot next door. Both men had taken to regularly feeding him carrots and runner beans. On his side, Adi had been forced to put up a whole new fence a few weeks previously when Ed had consumed most of the pea crop. He was a donkey on a mission, and Ed knew that at least one of the two men would have a carrot on him somewhere.

Shrieks of laughter came from the ground floor apartments. Marjorie's parties had taken off immediately once she'd joined the local WI group. A large package had arrived, and she and Sylvia were breaking it down into individual orders.
Marjorie and Sylvia planned to go and watch the fun-run with their husbands, and then distribute the packages to their rightful owners while the menfolk were still in the pub in the evening.
Marjorie was expecting no fewer than twenty-four ladies to turn up between six and seven O'clock.
Rachael would be collecting her packet later, when she came home from the television station.

Alan and Eileen were preparing too. The full moon was at 1.15 the next morning. They had a ritual to perform. They'd been performing the spell every night for the previous eight nights. Tonight was the climax. They couldn't risk a full fire in the woods and so Alan had purchased a small disposable barbecue. The hardest part for both of them was that the ritual required a blood sacrifice. "I'm not a ruddy Freemason. I'm not sacrificing any chickens." Alan had said frustratedly. "Well I'm not killing anything either." Eileen had stated emphatically.

They'd given the matter a great deal of thought. In the end, Alan had driven them both to Waitrose in Saltash. Luckily, the shop had been selling blood oranges. They could use one of those as their offering.

Denzel was preparing too. Dobson, sour faced as usual, and wearing his running gear, had just dropped off four envelopes. Each contained fifteen thousand pounds.
One was from Smugly, who didn't want to be revealed as the town underwear thief. One was from Dobson, who didn't want his unlawful activities made public either. John Dory was keen to ensure his relationship with Charity Sally didn't come under scrutiny.
Badcock had been the only one to make any real protest until Smugly had reminded him that if one went down, they'd all go down. Reluctantly, Badcock and Smugly had filled their envelopes. The money they used should rightfully have been sitting in the TWATS bank account.

Denzel had carefully placed the envelopes in the drawer of his desk in his unit at the Millpool. He didn't have a safe here, he didn't usually keep cash here anymore.
At one time, all his employees would be summonsed to the

unit at the Millpool, it was where they got paid and where the takings were deposited.
Denzel had moved all that part of his operation into his unit in town now.

He barely went to the Millpool these days, and it would have to be someone incredibly stupid who even thought of ripping him off. Denzel had connections, and a nasty reputation.

The Dutchman had instructed Denzel to collect the package from the yacht, and that one of his people would then accompany Denzel back to the shore where Denzel would hand over the cash.
The Dutchman had said it was important not to take large sums of money onto the yacht in case he was searched by customs any time. This made sense to Denzel. He never considered where on board the drugs might have been hidden.

For his part, Denzel didn't want the Dutchman to know where his real office was, and anyway, tomorrow afternoon he could bring the Doodlebug all the way up the river and avoid the people in town altogether.

Flood had said the same thing to Smugly and Cowboy too. He wanted to trap the vermin in their lairs and see what else they had hidden away.

As the sun dipped below the tree line at Kilminorth woods, Denzel locked the unit and began to walk along the river. He was heading for the mooring where his niece kept her brand-new boat.

Three pairs of eyes watch Denzel leave.

Cowboy and Uncle Keith stayed hidden in the bushes until the light had almost completely faded. Cowboy had no idea what he would find in Sprygellys unit, but he was certain the crook would have at least something of value. A short bit of crowbar work later, Cowboy and Keith were in possession of four brown envelopes stuffed full of notes.

From a different clump of bushes, Dobson cursed as he watched them leave. Those two clowns had just done exactly what he'd been planning to do. He hated Denzel's guts, and he wanted to see Denzel in as much hot water as possible. At this point, Dobson didn't know anything about the Dutchman, but just as Denzel had been keeping tabs on him, he'd been keeping tabs back since Sprygelly had tried to force his way into the TWATS.

Dobson decided to follow Cowboy and the flasher. From a safe distance, he tracked their quick progress along the riverbank, across the bridge, back up Station Road and finally, they disappeared into one of the sheds in the front garden at Emmety Villa. Dobson walked a little way up the hill and settled into a quiet spot in the garden of an empty house. He had to wait a long time before they came out again.

Dobson woke with a start. It was midnight and a clearly inebriated Cowboy and Uncle Keith were emerging from the shed. At the gate of Emmety Villa, they said a drunken goodnight to one another. Cowboy headed into town; Uncle Keith began the arduous climb up the hill towards his own house.

Dobson allowed them both a few minutes to leave, and then went to investigate the shed. The door was locked, but around the side, a window just large enough for Dobson to climb through, had been left slightly ajar. It was just too easy, he thought. It didn't take Dobson long to locate the cash, which the pair had evidently counted and was now sitting in an Aldi carrier bag on a table surrounded by an overflowing ashtray, an assortment of grubby looking mugs, and two empty, he guessed at the contents, vodka bottles?

Dobson pushed the carrier bag inside his hoodie. He slipped rapidly back out the way he'd come in. Rather than go back onto the road, he decided to go up the garden and cut through the wood. It was exactly the same route that Ed had used during his alpaca adventure. He was almost at the top when a noise from the wood startled him. He dived into the open flap of the poly tunnel and crouched down.

A figure, dressed much the same way as he was himself, emerged cautiously around the corner of the wall. The figure, Dobson guessed it was a man, looked around for a moment and then headed straight for the washing line where several pairs of Rachael's less than smalls dangled enticingly in the soft breeze.
Dobson felt a sharp pang of disappointment. Why hadn't

he seen them himself?

The figure deftly plucked the knickers from the line and stuffed them inside his hoodie. He had a quick look around to check there was no one there and dashed back up the slope. Before he disappeared under the trees, he had one last triumphant look at the garden. The full moon shone clearly on his face, and from Dobson's hiding place in the tunnel, he could see clearly, it was one of his fellow TWATS.
It was John Dory.
Dobson would never have thought the old codger could move so fast. He was impressed.

He decided to wait for Dory to clear the woods. Lowenna had been out every night for weeks and she'd almost caught Dobson half a dozen times. He stopped to take in his surroundings more fully. There was a stack of growbags at the end of the tunnel. He could use those he decided. He'd leave the money there, and collect it in the morning, just in case the Sargent was driving around again. He could explain away being out in his running gear, but there was no way he'd be able to explain £60'000 in used notes.

Trying to make as little noise as possible, he tipped the stack and left the carrier bag sandwiched between the bottom two bags.
He was about to leave for home, when yet another unexpected noise startled him. He crouched down again. Under the strong full moonlight, he watched Alan, in full Wizard regalia, and Eileen dressed in something quite similar but much more feminine. They made their way up the garden and then quietly disappeared into the woods. All Dobson could do was wait until they were gone.

The next ten minutes felt like an eternity. It was then that something new broke through the night. The distinct smell of paraffin from a disposable barbecue met Dobson's nostrils. He could hear a low chanting noise too.
His curiosity got the better of him, and he decided to go and look.

Under the trees, the disposable barbecue was burning cheerfully, and more importantly, safely.
Alan and Eileen were both naked and had their heads upturned and their eyes focussed on the night sky. They were both chanting. Alan Higginbottom had his back to Dobson, and now he bent over to retrieve something from the ground.
Dobson was horrified to get a full unobstructed view of Alans strawberry, and despite the cool temperature, his scrotum looked enormous.
Eileen was holding something which Alan now sliced into with the silver knife he'd just picked up.
Dobson was horrified as he saw blood spurt from Eileen's hands. She bent to pick up another of whatever it had been. The poor, poor creatures, Dobson thought.
The blood spurted again.
Both Higginbottom's were covered in it now. It trickled down their arms, it was on their chests, and it was even smeared onto their faces.
The chanting continued.
Dobson couldn't pull himself away now. What the hell was going on?

After another eternity, the chanting came to an end.

"That was great." Eileen said to Alan "Could you feel the energy?"

"That was awesome." Alan replied, and then, "Are you okay love?"
"I'm a bit sticky" came the answer.

Dobson had seen enough. He would get the money in the morning, and then he would never come back to Emmety Villa ever again.

He ran down the garden and made it home in a new record time.

The sun rose on a slumbering Looe. It was a Saturday, changeover day in high season. First the sky began to lighten over Rame Head, and by 5am it was light enough to read a book by.

The little birds began their day but the only dawn chorus most people heard was the seagulls revving up to another day of hunting for pasties. The noise was phenomenal. The residents were accustomed to it. Several of the visitors considered it most unreasonable. There was the occasional visitor who even thought that the town council could do something about it.
These were the same sort of people who said things like "I don't know what happened to the harbour, the last time I came, it was full of water" And "That rock sticking out of the water over there, does it go all the way to the bottom?"

Only a few vehicles moved around at 5am. Posties on their way to work, delivery drivers dropping off essential supplies to the cafes, cleaners, the early shift at the supermarket, and perhaps Veryan and Lowenna, but not this morning. Both women were tucked up in bed in their homes. Today would be a busy day. Every Saturday was. Today would be busier than usual.

The few remaining fishermen in the town followed hours that ran with the tides. Some mornings they went out at 5am, some mornings they were just coming home. This morning most were tied up and unloading. The gulls that circled the harbour went into an even louder frenzy of excited calling.

By 6am there were a few more people around. Hopeful visitors who'd made the overnight drive searched fruitlessly for somewhere to get breakfast. The full moon had pulled the tide up and so sea water was coming up through the grates in Fore Streets. The visitors got excited, the locals, knowing this was nothing unusual, just carried on as normal.

One or two embarrassed bodies stumbled along the street desperately regretting their lager induced liaisons of the night before. They had to get home before anyone else saw them. The walk of shame club who gathered at the taxi rank was larger than usual this morning. The full moon made people do all sorts of peculiar things.
The CCTV on the fish quay had no doubt recorded one or two of the incidents. Later that morning, the staff in the harbour office would cry tears of laughter as they witnessed who had been snogging who from behind the privacy of a stack of fish boxes.

The street cleaners began at 6am too. Unsung heroes who put the place back together again every single morning. Underpaid and underappreciated, without them, the place would have been ankle deep in chip cartons and Monster energy drink cans in no time. It was strange that these energy drinks didn't actually provide the users with enough get up and go to transport the empty can to a rubbish bin.

On the beach, Tony raked the sand and collected some of the debris from the previous evening while his colleague emptied overflowing bins and collected abandoned broken body boards and camping chairs.

At last, at 7am, the first of the shops began to open for bread and milk and newspapers. One or two made sales of fine quality park bench cider. Some of the locals were truly dedicated.

By eight o'clock, the first of the cafes began to allow people inside. The street was fuller now, but this was still mostly people going to work. In another hour, that would have transitioned into visitors.
By 10am, the streets and car parks would be crammed.

A busy summers day, a full moon, an event that would pull in hundreds of additional spectators as the mascot race broke down into the usual debacle, it was going to be a busy day.

For Denzel Sprygelly, it was going to be a memorable day.
For a very hung-over Uncle Keith and Cowboy, it was going to be a memorable day too.
For Ryan Smugly it was also going to be a memorable day.
But not for any of the reasons they'd anticipated.

Jimmy had discovered his boat was missing when he'd gone to check the moorings on his way to work. He was tearful when he'd rung the police to report it. Lowenna had gone on duty early and so she'd hopped in the car and gone down to the little supermarket to see him.
"We'll find it Jimmy" She'd reassured him. She felt sorry for him. There he was working his backside off in an extremely difficult, thankless job, and some knob had gone and stolen his most prized possession.

She was about to ring the coast guard office when her phone tinged with a message from Veryan.
"Can you get back here soon please? Something really important has come up."
Lowenna climbed back in the car, completed the one-way circuit of the town without squashing anyone, and drove back to the station. The car park was full of unmarked cars. Clearly, CID had come to town.

The briefing took almost two hours. Every one of Looe's regular attending constables had been brought in to hear it. Christopher Flood explained in detail what had been done so far, and what was about to happen. Lowenna and Veryan sat quietly through the entire presentation.
CID had indeed been busy. Christopher showed them slide after slide of Denzel Sprygelly, Ryan Smugly, Bill Dobson, Cowboy and Uncle Keith.
There were photographs of the comings and goings at the TWATS office, and at Denzel's, and at Emmety Villa.
"What is it about that place that keeps attracting the wrong-uns" Lowenna whispered to Veryan.

Christopher explained that the DI in charge of the drugs

bust, Bernard Flood, was expecting the targets to collect from the yacht anchored just offshore.

One or two of his officers, posing as the operatives of the Dutchman, would accompany each of the collectors back to the shore to collect payment. As soon as the money had changed hands, the collecting officers would then either arrest the targets or signal for assistance.
The whole operation would be supported by at least a dozen plain clothed officers based onshore.

Uniform branch was asked to continue with their day as normal, but not to do anything about the Doodlebug Denzel Sprygelly had been photographed stealing the night before.
He hadn't taken it very far. It was currently on the other side of the river and tied up to a ring on the quay, they revealed, covered with a filthy seagull spattered tarpaulin. They were asked not to do anything at all to interfere with any of the principle targets over the course of the day.
At around 5pm, it would be necessary for every available body to be on standby.

Lowenna pointed out that 5pm was the time the Mascot race was due to begin.
Rather than alarm any of the targets, it was decided to stand down two of the four uniformed officers who had been due to attend the event. They would be replaced with plain clothed officers from the CID team.

For the rest of the day, the CID team would continue to observe their targets.
Everything was arranged.

Afterwards in her office, Lowenna sat with DC Flood and Veryan and asked the questions both cousins had been wanting to ask.

"How long have you been working on this?"

Christopher explained that after the court case with Denzel and Maurice John Thomas, a serious complaint had been made about the influence the Special Club had in the town. Several prominent figures had been named; Ryan Smugly, John Dory, Bill Dobson and Alan Badcock, and of course Denzel.
Lowenna and Veryan understood this, there were a lot of people locally who resented the way the TWATS went about running their organisation.
Denzel had been making himself a target since he was a teenager. Denzel was also well known for using his Special Club status to manipulate things his way.
"But what about Cowboy and that other berk?" Veryan wanted to know.
Chris laughed.
After Maurice John Thomas was arrested, we left a couple of small cameras in there in case any of his old associates turned up. They didn't, but while he was supposed to be repairing the guttering, your bloke Cowboy let himself into the flat. He had a good rummage around and stole a teas maid and a jar of coffee, so we decided to follow him and see what else he got up to."

   "Oh!" was all the cousins could say. Chris continued. "One evening when we were here keeping an eye on Smugly, we followed him into the Marine Club, and Cowboy and his chum were at the bar boasting to a visitor that they could get hold of anything. They said they knew all about everything that goes on here. The boss suggested we approach Cowboy and see if we could draw him in. We sold him 50 dogs worm tablets and 50 ginseng pills." Chris stopped to laugh before continuing. "He thought they were ecstasy tablets and Viagra. Him and his mate have been selling them in town, along with several hundred bottles of vodka."

"Oh!" Said Lowenna and Veryan again. They hadn't been aware of any of this, and it had happened right under their noses.

Chris continued.

Once we've got them, we can lock them up for a while and squeeze them until they're dry. We checked their past, it's quite a record, for both of them."

Lowenna and Veryan knew this, but to date Cowboy had never been caught for anything serious. He was suspected of all sorts of things, but they'd never been able to get anything to stick.

Uncle Keith had somehow managed to avoid prosecution too.

"How the hell could all this happen without us knowing?" Lowenna wanted to know.

Veryan was indignant too. "This is crazy, if those two have been dancing around like this, it must have been visible?"

"It was." Chris offered "But don't beat yourselves up over it, we had to make sure it looked like everything was normal, so we kept you distracted."

Lowenna could feel her blood pressure beginning to rise. "And what exactly do you mean by that?"

Chris looked embarrassed. "You know all those underwear thefts? The ones in the villages?"

Lowenna could feel her temperature also rising now.

"Are you saying it was you lot all along?"

Chris quickly put his hands up to placate Lowenna. "Not at all" he said, "We just chucked in a few extra reports for the

villages whenever we needed you to be elsewhere."
"And the ones in town?" Lowenna was growling now. It wasn't that she was overly concerned about all the weeks she'd spent on nights. Lowenna wanted to know if it was CID who'd taken her knickers.
Christopher looked rightfully uncomfortable. The speed of his speech increased dramatically.
"Oh, they had nothing to do with us. We think they were all genuine incidents."
Lowenna relaxed a little. "And what did your investigations turn up about those then?" she said in a low menacing tone she usually reserved for teenagers.
Chris held his hands up in an open palm gesture. "Can't say for certain, but we think it might be one of the TWATS. They all go out in running gear at odd times."

Lowenna and Veryan already knew that Dobson was out late at night, but the knowledge the other three TWATS were also out and about was something new.
"Alan Badcock takes part in the Looe ten miler." Veryan said "and Dobson competes in anything and everything." Lowenna looked at her cousin and then at the young DC again. "From what I know, Ryan Smugly uses the gym at Pennyland most mornings, and John Dory goes swimming. He has done since his heart attack. Just how early were they out?"
"I'll need to check our logs." Was all that Chris could answer. "For now, we really need to focus on the job in hand."
That might be what you think, but I happen to have some arresting of my own."
Chris flinched and even Veryan was a little unsettled by the icy tone Lowenna used.

At just after eight o'clock, Bill Dobson's phone rang. He'd overslept. He swore as he fumbled to answer. Predictably, it was Smugly. "Bill, good morning." Smugly's voice oozed with his customary syrupy tones. He continued before Dobson could answer. "I need you to do something for me. I'll make it worth your while." Dobson snorted. The last time Smugly had made something worth his while, he'd given him a bottle of cheap Cote de Rhone, worth about £3.99. In return he'd picked Smugly up from Gatwick airport and driven him back to Cornwall. Smugly hadn't even paid for the fuel or the parking.

The trouble was Dobson needed Smugly. One day he would be chairman of the TWATS again, and to Dobson, that was tremendously important. Before he even knew what was going to be asked of him, Dobson had agreed. He swore again as he put the phone down. The carrier bag at Emmety Villa would have to wait until this evening. At least he knew a bit more about what was going on now.

Morning passed into afternoon. In the town, fish and chips were consumed by the lorry load. Blue ice creams were slurped and then regurgitated onto pavements and roads.

The bars were doing a roaring trade as holiday makers crammed inside to escape from the sun and the fresh sea air. In the Beach Shack, dozens of pairs of knickers were sold. They bore the legend 'If you can smell my pasty, you'm too close!'

The beach was packed, the streets were full, and the trainloads of animal print clad visitors kept arriving and vomiting their loads onto the platform to add to the throng.

Jimmy and his team ran on caffeine and sheer nervous energy in order to make it through another challenging day.

Paul Sprygelly served cold beers and cream teas to customers who'd come in to use the hotel bar. At 4pm he had to stop serving. Leonard had said he was unwilling to run in the Lugworm suit this year, and anyway, he'd already done more than his hours for the week.
Paul knew he couldn't press the issue and that Leonard was perfectly correct in stating that, 64 hours in five days, was enough.
There wasn't a single member of staff who couldn't tell a similar story. Paul was going to have to run the race himself.

Donald and Sylvia were getting ready to go out. They planned to go and have a cream tea somewhere before the race began. Donald couldn't decide what to wear. "What about these?" he held up a pair of sand-coloured chinos.

"You can if you like, but I think the Alan Whicker look has finished now dear." came the reply. Donald carried on looking through the rail. "Well, I can't wear shorts, it'll look silly. Ruddy things." He stopped his perusal of trousers and turned to face Sylvia. "I used to put on Tubular Bells, these days I only ever put on tubular bloody bandages." He was about to say something about Sylvias outfit. He decided better of it. That was a lot of leopard print. If she got mixed up with a crowd from Plymouth, she'd be so well camouflaged, he'd have trouble finding her again. This had already happened once this week.
Sylvia tugged down her top momentarily to flash her boobs at Donald. "Want a go mister?"
At 74 now, Donald wished she would stop doing that.

Norman and Marjorie were in the garden talking across the fence to Adi. Ed the Donkey had come to join them. He didn't say much, but he followed the conversation intently while he waited for someone to produce a carrot.
Adi had suggested they watch the first part of the race from the terrace at the Rivercroft Hotel. "You can sit outside above the level of the road, you'll have a good view of a large part of the course there, the beer is cheap, and it's probably one of the nicest bars in town. They don't tolerate assholes in there either." Adi finished.
"We'll go and have a look." Norman thanked him and he and Marjorie held hands as they walked back down the steps.
Adi watched them go. Marjorie had been wearing zebra stripped leggings today. "What do you reckon to them then buddy?" he asked the inquisitive donkey. Ed didn't have an opinion, mostly he was interested in carrots.

At 4pm, a beautiful white yacht sailed gracefully into the

waters about a third of a mile off Looe beach and dropped anchor. Keen photographers took pictures of her while lobster-coloured sunbathers fantasised about an adventure on something similar.

At the same time, Lowenna and Veryan checked that all the barriers that would curtail the traffic were in place. The Lions had done their usual efficient job and all the signage and bodies that would be needed to use it were where they were supposed to be. Closing a public highway was a complicated matter and both Lowenna and the chief of the Lions had to sign off the legal documents which allowed them to do so. At last, everything was in place.

On the quayside, the runners began to assemble. Most left the pulling on of their costumes until the last possible minute.

On the yacht, Bernard Flood waited patiently and monitored his team via their phones and radios. The coastguard was on standby in case any of the three intended pickups decided to take an alternative route.

As five O'clock approached, a Doodlebug made its way along the river and past the end of the Banjo pier. The tide was high enough to have pushed several hundred people off the beach now, and those people were finding places to watch the race from. The Doodlebug turned west just after the white rock and began a circuit of the island. At least a dozen pairs of binoculars followed its progress.

From a van on the car park, a PA announced that the race would begin in ten minutes. Would all competitors please make their way to the start?

Lowenna and Veryan were already there. Cousin Paul had been dropped off by a taxi. He was hot already. Leonard was right, the head piece stank.
A veritable array of sea creatures made their way towards the start line while continuing to adjust their heavy outfits. Derek the Dolphin was there, so was Ollie the octopus. "Look" whispered Veryan "It's cousin Polly. Polly the Ollie."
It wasn't in the least bit funny but both Lowenna and Veryan were so tense they were almost on the verge of hysteria. The drug squad might be busting a few people tonight, but more importantly to Veryan and Lowenna, they were probably going to find out who'd been stealing their undies for months.

Larry the Looe Lobster waddled by, followed swiftly by Colin the Crab, who in an ingenious move by the designers of the suit, could only move sideways. Winnie the Whelk had fallen over and was having to be helped back onto her feet by the Springfield Starfish and the rather distressed looking Sea Vista Seaweed. That one had been dreamt up even later than Lenny the Lugworm.

Mavis the Mackerel came rushing down the street, she'd finished her shift late and the taxi had been forced to drop her on the bridge now the road was closed.

The Polperro Porpoise appeared to be in hot pursuit. Rita the Razorfish was shaking her shells at Mike the Muscle, who shook his back.

Lowenna hoped there wasn't going to be any trouble between those two again this year and said as much to Veryan.

"We're still missing some" Veryan answered. Both women became aware of a vehicle trying to work its way along the quay. It was the Looe Lions bus. It came to a stop beside them and out tumbled Chloe the Cockle, Walter the Winkle and the imaginatively named Dave the Dogfish.

Corinne the Clam emerged from the fish market where she'd just swallowed an impressive glass of wine. Her decorative flange flapped freely at the crowd.

The announcer called again, and the crowd parted in a few places to let through a seal, a herring gull, a basking shark, an otter, something that might have been a heron, a puffin and lastly a rather unpleasant looking conger eel.

As the clock ticked down the last few second, the competitors jostled one another at the starting line. The town clock struck, the hooter was blasted, and the Mascots began their tortuous plod around Looe to the excited cheering of the crowds. The noise was deafening.

Bill Dobson pulled the little boat alongside the yacht and held a short rope ladder as a man descended. The man was carrying a rucksack which he handed wordlessly to Dobson. Dobson let go of the rope and began the journey back around the island before heading back up the river to a place on the quay.

As Dobson came back up the river, he saw the familiar detestable figure of Denzel Sprygelly leaving the harbour in a boat almost identical to the one Smugly had instructed him to use. Any other time, Dobson would have given Denzel a two-finger salute, but he was sweating now. He needed to get this bloke, whoever he was, to the TWATS office. Dobson was in way over his head, and he knew it.

He tied the boat up by the fish market and the two began to climb one of the ladders that was set into the wall. Because of the race, there was a bar on the fish market tonight, it was crowded with enthusiastic drinkers. Someone had set up a sound system. Hot Water by Level 42 was playing.

As he looked behind him to see if his passenger was following him up the ladder, another Doodlebug went putting by. This time it was Cowboy and Uncle Keith.

Dobson was still dithering and watching the Doodlebug when his passenger reached the top.
"Let's get on with it." the man urged. Dobson turned sharply and began to push his way through the crowd. If he'd had anywhere to run to, he would have. The capable looking man who was following put paid to any idea of that, he was probably carrying a gun or some other type of weapon. Dobson did his best to shut out visions of how

this nightmare was going to end.
Unseen by Dobson, the police officer behind him had nodded to acknowledge two of his colleagues. They had predicted Smugly would use the TWATS office rather than his own home. They were correct. All three now followed Dobson's stumbling steps.

On the quay, Sylvia and Donald were enjoying the spectacle immensely. They'd had a delicious cream tea and a bottle of prosecco at the little café on the seafront. Sylvia was feeling the effect of the wine now and was loving it. Donald was happy too. The race was thoroughly entertaining. They'd never had anything remotely like this back home. He caught his thoughts. This was home now. Later he'd be spending an enjoyable evening with his new friend Norman. They'd decided to go to the place Adi had suggested. Norman and Marjorie were already there.

Just in front of them, a giant dolphin and a rather large porpoise were jostling for first place. Without warning, and with no concern whatsoever about any witnesses in the spectators, the dolphin turned towards the porpoise and barged him straight into the crowd. The porpoise hit the tarmac with an audible thud. The dolphin threw back his head and laughed and then glided off again.

Lowenna and Veryan had seen the whole thing. "Looks like they're starting early this year." Lowenna said to her cousin. "Oh dear" Veryan replied "I hope they don't all kick off again like last year."
"I have a feeling they might." Lowenna answered. She was right, and at that stage she still didn't know that Denzel had paid at least half a dozen of the runners to do just that.

The crowd helped get the porpoise upright again. Lowenna and Veryan did their best to keep up with the clutch of shellfish who were between them and the dolphin.

They didn't see the next incident when behind them, the Looe Lobster deliberately tripped up the Colin the Crab.

Ryan Smugly, almost as devious and scheming as Denzel, had made sure that Badcock and Dory were at the TWATS office waiting for Dobson to arrive. Smugly was loath to share any profit, but he knew that if he involved them now, he'd be able to manipulate them for the rest of their miserable lives.

He'd explained to them that by borrowing some of the TWATS funds for a few weeks, they were all going to become exceedingly rich. Badcock and Dory, little pound note signs burning like fires in their bloodshot eyes, hadn't even asked what was involved. Smugly could have been selling grannies into slavery and they'd have gone along with it. As long as it made them a profit, that was where their morality ended.

Consequently, the pile of money sitting on the desk in the TWATS administration office, had all their fingerprints on it. Later, CID would be delighted. At this moment though, the trio were busy congratulating themselves, yet again, on their own cleverness. Two of the fools didn't even know what they were involved in.

They heard the main door open and the usual heavy breathing that was one of Dobson's trademarks, as he stomped up the stairs. Another set of footsteps joined Dobson's.

None of the TWATS heard the door click as the two officers from the fish quay were now joined by another three of their colleagues, who quietly let themselves in behind Dobson.

Dobson had barely set foot inside the admin room when the remaining CID caught up. All the colour drained from the faces of the four TWATS as warrant cards were displayed and rights were read.

Christopher Flood arrived just as handcuffs were being slapped on.
He dipped his hand into the rucksack Dobson had dropped and pulled out one of four well wrapped packages.
He lifted the packet to his nose and gave a long sniff.
"Ah, Columbia's finest." Dory and Badcock both took sharp inhalations"
Christopher sniffed it again and then said, "Bloody good coffee this." He winked at Smugly.
Dobson fainted.
Smugly burst into tears.

Badcock and Dory began protesting that they knew nothing about it.
DC Flood drew their attention to two tiny cameras fitted on the decorative plasterwork on the ceiling and another discreetly attached to the board that listed all the former chairmen.
"Oh, I think we can prove that you do." was all he said.

The unhappy gang of four were led out to the waiting marked police cars.
A lot of local people witnessed the event. Within ten minutes, the word had spread to the furthest reaches of the town. Facebook was alive with speculation. Some of the posts suggested the TWATS had been involved in a plot to assassinate the Queen. A few posts speculated on the recent underwear thefts. After fifteen minutes, the foursome had been accused of just about every crime there was, and to be truthful, some of those accusations had mileage.

Things were getting stroppy on the quay. Cuthbert the Conger Eel, for no apparent reason, had taken a swing at Lenny the Lugworm. Paul was sweating heavily inside the outfit. All he wanted to do was complete the course and get the bloody thing off again.

When Cuthbert took a swing at the back of his head, he'd been completely unprepared for it and had gone crashing into the table at the watering station. Luckily, as in most of the incidents, the suit had absorbed most of the force of the blow. The table was not so lucky. Bottles of water and cups of refreshingly chilled glucose drinks went spattering into the surrounding crowd.
Paul lost his footing and landed in a crumpled mess which then caused a further pile up as the otter, Walter the Winkle and Dave the Dogfish all stumbled into one another to make an untidy heap.

On the water, Denzel had the throttle fully open and was rapidly approaching the yacht. Cowboy and Uncle Keith had rounded the end of the Banjo pier a little too fast. The force of the incoming wave which hit them, had rocked the boat so much that Keith, who had been standing to get a better view, was sent hurtling into the water. It was lucky that Cowboy heard him shriek otherwise Keith would have had to have swum back to the Banjo on his own. Cowboy killed the throttle and circled back around to help the bedraggled flasher get back on board.
Denzel was very pleased with himself as he accepted his rucksack. As before with Dobson, a man climbed down the ladder into the Doodlebug. "Let's go and get the money then shall we?" the man pointed back towards Looe beach and the entrance to the harbour.
"No problemo." Denzel began to head back in the

direction indicated.

On the racetrack, things were becoming all the more fractious. The Starfish and the Olli the Octopus were swinging tentacles at one another in a clear attempt to inflict damage. It looked impressive, but really it was all quite ineffectual, as most of the tentacles didn't have any oomph behind them.
Winnie the Whelk was on the ground grappling with Corinne the Clam. Now, both their decorative flanges were flapping around at the crowd.
At the very back, the otter was having an argument with someone in the crowd who'd inadvertently stepped out in front of him.
Paul, still running as Lenny the Lugworm, and the Porpoise, were back on their feet and doing their damndest to catch up with the Dolphin and the Conger eel which had assaulted them.
The two CID officers who had been seconded to the race, were behind Veryan and Lowenna breaking up yet another fight, this time a threesome of Dave the Dogfish, Mavis the Mackerel and Rita the Razorfish were all trying to batter one another.

Lowenna gave the puffin a shove as it slowed down beside her.
"Just get on with it," she growled "and no bloody nonsense or I'll be clipping your wings too."
She turned to Veryan. "You'd better call the reinforcements in; this is getting out of hand."

The reinforcements were the volunteer lions. Veryan fished her phone from her pocket and sent a quick text to the marshals.

The marshals, in their Lions' tabards, quickly stepped into calm things down. All this succeeded in doing was making things worse.
Sea creatures and Lions now began to argue with one another.

Lowenna stopped trying to catch up with the Dolphin and the Conger eel. She pointed at Colin the Crab.
"I think this years Colin is pissed Veryan."
"How do you know that?" Veryan answered.
"Well just look at him, he's going forwards."

Denzel went straight up the river and under the bridge. Where the East and West Looe rivers met, he turned westward and kept going until he was almost at the slipway. He carefully brought the little boat up to the wall.
Denzel turned to his passenger. "Can you grab that rope?" He pointed at a mooring line attached to a block by the slipway. It was only then that he looked over to the door of his unit, and saw it hanging open and splintered.
Denzel panicked. As the CID officer lent for the rope, Denzel gunned the engine. The little boat shot forward, and just as with Uncle Keith a short time earlier, the CID officer completely lost his balance and was sent headfirst into the water.

Denzel checked to see he still had the rucksack. It was there sitting safely in the bow of the little boat. Before the CID officer could get to his feet in the shallow water, Denzel, his heart, if he had such a thing, pounding in his chest, headed back to where the rivers met. Denzel knew two things for certain. He needed to get off the boat, and he needed to hide.

Back at the slipway, a pair of plain clothes CID had arrived to assist their waterlogged colleague. "Just look at that." Said one of them, "He's one of them soggy bottom boys." "Come on Jimbo, this is no time to be going for a swim" quipped the other.
Jimbo waded out of the water and laughed at his own predicament. "The tracker is still working isn't it?"
Both officers checked their phones. The tracker was indeed switched on. Denzel, or rather the bugged rucksack, was currently heading towards the police station.

Cowboy and Uncle Keith arrived at the yacht and the Dutchman lowered them a rucksack on a rope.

"Hold steady while my associate here climbs down." he instructed them.

Cowboy had no such intention, and the minute Uncle Keith had the rucksack in his hands, Cowboy opened the throttle and the two made a beeline for Millendreath beach. The officer who'd been halfway down the short rope ladder clambered back up again.

"Well now, that was predictable" he said to Flood who nodded and answered saying. "Wasn't it. That was exactly what we'd watched them rehearsing."

Waiting in a car overlooking the beach were four CID officers. "Wait until they tie up on the jetty" Flood instructed them over the radio. "Make sure they're right on the sand before you intervene."

The DI put down his radio and picked up his binoculars. "Oh, hang on a minute" he sputtered; the buggers are running to Plaidy."

Flood snatched up his radio again. "All available units, Cowboy and the freak are heading for Plaidy, please respond."

There was an uncomfortable pause and then a chorus of voices came back.

"On it Gov."

"We'll be right there."

"Got a line on him but it'll be a few minutes Gov'ner"

Flood was getting agitated now and his team could hear it in his voice.

"Chris, how are things at your end?"

"Four TWATS in handcuff here dad, sorry, boss." Came the reply.

"Good, well done lad, get me the rib and get me back

onshore quick as you can, will you?"
"Roger that boss."

"Unit two, have you got that slippery bastard now?"
There was a pause. "He's managed to get away from us, but we've got him on the tracker. Davy and Rob are on it. He's on the river heading towards the railway station boss."
"Make sure you get him before he can dump that rucksack." Flood snapped back. After all that work, it would be infuriating if Denzel Sprygelly got away once again.

Veryan and Lowenna had split up and were quietly reading the riot act to the assorted sea creatures.
"You are going to go straight to the finish line and you're going to wait for me right there." Lowenna instructed the Looe Lobster before moving on to the Heron.
Veryan was giving similar instructions. "Get around to the shed, finish the course, and don't even think about going anywhere until I say you can go!" She sent Mike the Muscle and Cyril the Seagull on their way to finish the route.

Both Veryan and Lowenna knew that if they stopped the race altogether, there would be a riot. At the moment, the route was lined by good humoured, only slightly drunk spectators. All that could change very quickly.
Lowenna and Veryan wanted this part of the day to be over. While all the race shenanigans were occurring, they'd had text messages to tell them about the TWATS arrest. Lowenna wanted to make sure she spoke to them before they were hauled off to more permanent accommodation.

Cowboy and Uncle Keith hit Plaidy beach like a scene from D-Day. No sooner did the boat crunch into the shingle, than Cowboy was over the side and clutching the rucksack, trying frantically to scrabble up through the sand and gravel. It was like watching a hamster on an enormous wheel. His limbs flapped frantically, but he made hardly any progress. Another thump behind him and Keith was floundering in the shingle too. Cowboy tried to lunge forward and dropped the rucksack into a foot of water. He just managed to grab it before a wave snatched it away.
"What about the boat?" Keith gasped.
"Don't worry about it." Cowboy called back over the noise of the waves. "Someone we know is bound to grab her when they see her. We'll get it back tomorrow. Right now, we need to get away from that boat." He jerked a thumb back at the 'Dutchman's' yacht.
"If we can just keep our heads down for a couple of hours, I reckon we'll be fine."
Keith, in an unusual spot of quick thinking answered. "I reckon if we call the drug squad and say he's there, they'll get him off our backs." Keith attempted to dip into the pocket of his sodden jeans. He was surprised to learn that his phone wasn't working.
"Let's get back to the shed." Cowboy was eager to get off the beach.

Fifty puzzled sunbathers watched as Cowboy and Keith abandoned the Doodlebug and made their arduous way up through the loose, sucking sand. By the time the first of the CID cars had arrived, Cowboy and Keith had vanished. The tracker in the rucksack, damaged by the seawater, had stopped working.

The scene at the race varied according to which of the

competitors could be seen. Lowenna's assessment of Colin the Crab had been correct, and to the surprise of the crowds, he'd decided to pop into the Looe River View Hotel for a beverage. If you've ever watched a crab trying to climb a flight of steps, you'll realise how futile this was. What really rubbed salt in the wound was that as he sat at the bottom sulking, Walter the Winkle was up them in a thrice.

Paul, intent on defending the honour of his hotel, had finally caught up with Cuthbert. The Conger eel towered over the lugworm, and to the spectators, it looked like a futile contest. Luckily for him, Paul had the advantage. He was hot, he was tired, he was emotionally fried from his job at the hotel, and he was ready to let it all out.
He put his head down and ran straight for the Conger who was waggling aggressively at him. Cuthbert attempted an evasive move, but at the last second, Lenny the Lugworm stumbled on a speed hump. The two came together with an audible squelch. The momentum sent them both off the edge of the quay and into the water with such a splash that the crowd cheered as if it was 1966.

"Oh, sod it." Lowenna swore so loudly, the cheering closest to her came to an abrupt stop. It just wasn't becoming of a police officer, especially a female police Sargent, to use that sort of language.
"Veryan." She called "I'm going to have to go in and get these dickheads out." The crowd gasped. "They'll never swim in those outfits."
Lowenna was about to ditch her jacket when one of the RNLI ribs arrived and four sets of capable hands began dragging the conger eel and the lugworm back out of the water.

"You bloody heroes!" Lowenna shouted to them. The crowd gasped again. One woman shouted that she was going to write to her MP. Lowenna shouted back. "You go ahead love, knock yourself out. At this point in history, I really couldn't give a toss." The crowd, except for the MP woman, cheered.

At the finish line, a huge cheer went up as Winnie the Whelk had crossed the finish line and won.
A little way back by the bridge, the Dolphin and the Porpoise were now having a full-blown punch up. Lowenna had had enough.
"Veryan love, you're in charge. Arrest both those idiots, put handcuffs on their flippers if you have to. I'm going back to the station."

Denzel had abandoned the Doodlebug and had clambered up the riverbank and across the railway line. It didn't look like anyone was following him. He could hear a helicopter somewhere close. It might have been the air ambulance, or a film crew following the mascot race from the air. On the other hand, it might be someone else. He'd looked back to see his soaked former passenger being helped out of the river by two men. Things were clearly not what they seemed. Denzel's rat senses had served him well in the past. Right now, he needed to hide while he thought about his next move. That's what cornered rats did. He dashed across the road and dived into the woods.

The trio of police officers back at the Millpool watched the tracker on the screens of their phones as it moved into the trees.

DI Flood was on land now. The yacht had done its job, so he'd sent the crew back to the Barbican.

They'd lost the signal for the rucksack Cowboy and Uncle Keith were carrying, but the police helicopter had picked up two men heading up to the area of Looe also known as the Barbican. Flood had told the helicopter crew to observe from the maximum distance. He had a fairly good idea where they were heading anyway.

The news on the tracker Sprygelly had, suggested he was heading towards the same place.

Lowenna had arrived back at the police station. Smugly was the last of the four to have his fingerprints taken. His three accomplices sat mutely on a bench in the booking room. Lowenna, after a quick chat with her CID colleagues, entered the room. Smugly was sitting now too.

Lowenna's entry was like the arrival of the head of school. All four men hung their heads, afraid to meet her gaze.

"Right then you lot." Lowenna began pacing.
"I know all about your drug operation." She paused for a minute to see if there was any response before continuing. "And I know all about your other activities."
In truth, at this point, she didn't, but they didn't need to know that.
"So, I'm going to ask you a single QUESTION!" she barked the last word so sharply that DC Christopher Flood and three of his colleagues almost spilled their coffees.
Dobson began crying.
"Look at me when I'm talking to you!" she barked again. Four heads jerked up and Lowenna stopped to scrutinise each of the sorry looking faces.
"Which one of you bastards has been stealing my KNICKERS?" Lowenna shouted so loudly the bars on the window rattled.
All four TWATS stood up.

Cowboy and Uncle Keith had made it to the top of Looe Barbican by cutting through people's gardens and then slipping along a hedge line in the fields behind the primary school. They came to more houses at a small close called Baydown. The Barbican pub sat enticingly on the opposite side of the road.
Cowboy, confident that no one was following, looked at Keith and panted "I'm knackered, do you fancy a pint?" Keith, never one to refuse nodded enthusiastically. "I'm still a bit moist mate, can you bring me one out?"
"Yeah alright then."
"Put them on my slate." Keith told Cowboy.
"They let you have a slate?" Cowboy was astonished. Keith was his best mate, but he wouldn't have lent him a fiver even if Keith had won the lottery, he was so unreliable. They crossed the road and Cowboy went into the bar to

order.

They spent a pleasant hour there before deciding to continue their journey, some four pints each later.

Denzel meanwhile had been carefully working his way through the woods. After what felt like a lifetime, he came to a place where the trees parted and gave way to a small paddock. Ed the donkey heard Denzel approaching and looked up hopefully.

Denzel had a new idea. He'd read all about the Donkey and the alpacas in the Cornish Times. He put the rucksack down and slipped between the wires into the donkey field. It only took a few seconds and Ed's tether was undone. Denzel ventured a little further down the paddock and made sure the gate was open.

"Now you go and have some fun my little friend." He gave the donkey a shove on his rump. Ed didn't budge.

Denzel didn't have time to waste so he assumed that Ed would find his way out on his own. If there were any police around, the donkey would keep them occupied.

He retrieved the rucksack, and unnoticed by anyone, slipped down the steps to the old stable building where Cowboy and Keith had stored the vodka. The door was locked but a quick look around allowed Denzel to spot the open window that Bill Dobson had crawled through the night before.

It took a bit of effort to squeeze his paunch through, but with a lot of wriggling and huffing and puffing, he finally managed to get through, landing on his hands in a mess of dog ends, vodka caps and a spread of grime.

He would wait here until the next morning. It would be uncomfortable, but no worse than prison had been.

As his eyes adjusted to the light, he noticed the stack of crates loaded with the salvaged vodka.
"The thieving bastard!" he uttered; the irony of his statement entirely lost on him. Those were his crates. Then he spotted the discarded envelopes on the floor.
Denzel knew exactly who had broken the door of his unit open now.
When he caught up with Cowboy, noses were going to bleed.

Denzel ducked reflexively as a babble of voices outside announced a taxi unloading. The voices were familiar. It was some of his older relatives. What on earth were they doing here?
Denzel recognised auntie Val. What on earth was she doing out? She was eighty-nine and could barely walk. That sounded like auntie Maureen too, she was in her nineties.
A third voice was clearly that of his sister.
The voices faded as the three ladies climbed the steps to go and collect their intimate purchases from Marjorie.

Taxis kept arriving, Denzel recognised a lot of the voices. It sounded like whatever was going on was something akin to a gathering of the nearly departed. If he'd known why, he'd have been horrified.

A key scraped in the lock, and before Denzel could duck out of sight, Cowboy had stepped inside, rapidly followed by Uncle Keith.

For a few seconds, all they could do was stare at one another.
"You bastard." Denzel growled in the voice he generally used to sack people. He bent to pick up one of the

envelopes.

"It wasn't me." Came Cowboys rather frail attempt at denial.

"Shut the door." Denzel ordered Uncle Keith. Uncle Keith obediently did as he was told.

"Explain this to me." Was Denzel's next command. It was then that he spotted the rucksack Cowboy had draped over his shoulder.

Another car could be heard pulling up outside. Probably another taxi Denzel thought. Then another one arrived. The sound of hurried footsteps slapped on the steps. Whoever it was, was probably late for the ready to meet God party he thought.

"You're going to give that bag to me" Denzel continued, I know you've got my money." He waved the empty envelope for dramatic effect.

"Pah" snorted Cowboy, your moneys right…."

He stopped abruptly as he realised the money wasn't where he'd left it. He snorted again.

"You spannering wanker" he spat venomously at Sprygelly, "You've already had it. In case you hadn't noticed, there's two of us."

Denzel tossed his head back and laughed.

"You think I'm afraid of your and you girlfriend?" he pointed contemptuously at Keith.

There was an almighty crash as DI Bernard Flood booted the door.

Before Denzel or Cowboy and Keith could react, the old stable was full of CID officers.

Another car, this time a marked one with blue lights flashing, pulled up. Veryan and Lowenna climbed out and made their way up to their colleagues.

Upstairs in Marjorie's, twenty panicked old ladies made a

rapid exit and attempted to flee the scene before they could be questioned.
Not understanding what was going on, Lowenna called out "Stop them." The panicked old dears were doing their best to clamber over fences and get to the safety of the woods. Christopher Flood and his unoccupied cohorts jumped to it and got busy apprehending the startled retirees.
"Can I see what's in the carrier bag please he asked Denzel's auntie Valerie. He quickly began to wish he hadn't.

In the poly tunnel, Ed looked up from the courgettes he was feasting on. There were a lot of people in the garden now. Perhaps one of them would have a carrot.

By the time Donald and Norman got back from the pub, everyone had gone. Jimmy and Rachael were delighted to hear the news that their beloved little boat had been found, and were upstairs celebrating, privately. Adi had discovered Ed was missing from his paddock again. He was relieved to learn that Ed had only gone as far as the poly tunnel next door. Then he remembered the cannabis plants.

Ed was happy. He was full of courgettes. He wasn't sure what those stinging nettle type things were, and he hadn't liked the smell, so he'd left them alone.
Adi knocked on Donald's door to apologise. Donald quickly fetched Norman. The trio walked hurriedly back up the garden to inspect the damage.
Aside from the courgettes, everything else was exactly as it had been in the morning, oh, apart from the stack of grow bags they noticed. Ed had obviously pushed the pile over. They decided that could wait until the morning.

After they said goodnight and their doors had clicked. Alan, who had watched the whole pantomime, decided to go and have a look himself.
A few minutes later he let himself back into the flat. He was holding a carrier bag.
He was beside himself with excitement.
"Eileen, come and look at this, the magic, it worked!

# Epilogue

The day that Denzel was sent to prison, Cowboy, Keith, Smugly, Dobson, Dory and Badcock were also sent down. The whole town breathed a huge sigh of relief.

DI Bernard Flood was walking along the street to meet Veryan and Lowenna.
Where one of the bakeries once stood, there was a new shop. It sold and hired fancy dress outfits apparently. The owner, Alan, was incredibly proud of it. It had a simple sign over the big window. It said Mr Benn's in big purple letters. On the door was a sign that said This way for adventures. Alan was wearing the wizard outfit.
After all the trials he'd gone through, Alan was blissfully happy.

# The Arrival of Regit.
## Jeremy Moorhouse

Regit hadn't planned to come to Earth and certainly not to Chippenham, but now he's here for a few days, he might as well find out a bit more about these peculiar Bipeds and their strange habits and customs.

Phillip and Kelly and their neighbour Lucy are left with dozens of questions when Regit arrives in their midst. Why does he keep dressing like different pop stars from the 1980's? Where does he go when he disappears? Does he really eat cat biscuits? Who redecorated the bathroom?

Moley saw Regit arrive. He has some questions too. Major Thompson of the 'Special unit' also has questions.

Crop circles, Adam Ant, Big cat sightings in the countryside It's all going on.
Follow Regit as he tries to make sense of our crazy world.

"An absorbing flight of imagination based on a sound philosophy of how good life could be.
A fun-filled lark underpinned by environmental awareness and a knowledge of the old English landscape and the mystical secrets of the country's ancient sites. A very enjoyable read with some laugh-out-loud moments.
Good Stuff.

# Blocked!
## Jeremy Moorhouse

Miranda has a superpower, but she doesn't know she has it. What began as a bit of fun for relaxation has become a reality.
Miranda 'blocks' people who annoy her, and they disappear without a trace.
But where do they go? What are the consequences? And what happens if Miranda has to Un-block somebody?

With a cast of characters you'll recognise from any small town, and their spirit guides, Marc Bolan, Mata Hari, and Norman Wisdom to name just a few, laugh your way through Miranda's journey of discovery.
You'll love it!

# The Twelve Groans of Christmas.
## Jeremy Moorhouse

Christmas had it coming!

We all know somebody who doesn't enjoy the festive season, right?
Well, this book is for that person.
You'll recognise the characters, you might even wince as you remember when that particular thing happened to you.
What you'll most certainly do, is laugh.

"I laughed so much at this I bought copies of it for everyone at work.
Jeremy Moorhouse, you make me howl!"

Jeremy Moorhouse.

You can find out more about Jeremy Moorhouse on his Facebook page, Author and Storyteller, Jeremy Moorhouse.

If this offering has made you laugh, please leave a review on Amazon or the Facebook page. Thank you.

Printed in Great Britain
by Amazon